The Day Trip

Also by the same author

Up the Square

A L Craig

The Day Trip

Naylor Publishing

Copyright © 2000 Andrew Craig

The right of Andrew Craig to be identified
as the author of the work has been asserted by him
in accordance with the Copyright, Designs and
Patents Act 1988

All of characters in this publication
are fictitious, and any resemblance to
real persons, living or dead,
is purely coincidental.

All rights reserved. No part of this publication
may be reproduced, stored in a retrieval system,
or transmitted, in any form or means without the
prior written permission of the publisher, nor be
otherwise circulated in any form of binding or
cover other than that in which it is published
and without a similar condition being imposed
on the subsequent purchaser.

Published in Great Britain by
Naylor Publishing

ISBN 0-9538533-0-6

Printed and bound in Great Britain by
Alphagraphics Leeds

To Carron, Derek + family

Dedicated to my dearest nana.

Thanks for everything
Andrew.

Weardale slang

ar nar . . . . I know
nar . . . . no
divent . . . . don't
ar divent nar . . . . . I don't know
whey . . . . .well
champion . . . . fine
ar's champion . . . . I'm fine
gan . . . . go
ar's ganning . . . . . .I'm going
canna . . . . can't
get thee pipe . . . . .wait a minute
nee . . . . no
arraway . . . . go away

Chapter 1

August came in as July went out, with no let up in the beautiful sunny weather. Apart from a thunderstorm the week previously, Alistair hadn't seen any rain at all during the three weeks he'd been staying at his nana's in Stanhope.

This summer of 1963 in Weardale in the north east of England, was certainly turning out to be no damp squib – much to Alistair's delight. There was no place on earth as lovely, especially on long summer days. You could keep your tropical islands – Stanhope was his paradise.

'Are ye two getting up today or are yer glued to that mattress? It's half past eight mind!' shouted nana up the stairs.

'I'm awake!' called Alistair. 'Five minutes an' I'll be down nana!'

'Whey, give Roy a shake will yer? That bugger'll sleep the clock round given the chance!'

Roy was Alistair's cousin. At fourteen he was two years older than him.

'Ha way, time to get up Rip Van Winkle,' said Alistair, shaking Roy. 'Nana's shouting – Breakfast's nearly ready.'

'Eh . . . what . . . ? Orh, yer broke me dream man.'

'What dream was it this time? Were yer being crowned king of England?'

'Nar, better than that man. It was a woman . . . a beautiful blonde . . . aboot twenty years old to be more specific. Ar'd just wined an' dined her at Jo Jo's cafe – by candlelight of course. We were the only ones in there – me an' this gorgeous bird, holding hands across one of the tables. You weren't there, or any of the local rabble.'

'Oh yeah, an' what did yer have for yer dinner? One of Betty's hotdogs an' a bottle of Coca-Cola to wash it down with? You certainly know how to treat a woman, don't you?'

'Actually, yer clever little Yorkshire git – there was quite an extensive menu. You could choose from soup in a basket, scampi in yer hanky, or corn on yer cobs. I ordered two massive steaks though, ar thought she'd need building up, ganning out with the Stanhope Stud like. We finished off with Irish coffee and cigars, an' before yer ask – yes, she did smoke a cigar. One of these modern, equality type women yer nar. Not modern enough to pay half the bill though – ar paid Betty – left her a five pund tip. Yer should've seen her, bowing an' scraping an' holding the door open fer us as we left. Ar bet she'd wet her knickers. Anyway, we left and strolled hand in hand by the riverside, the moonlight shining down on us . . . '

'An what happened next?' asked Alistair in anticipation.

'Whey, ar was just ganning to tek her round the back o' the band hut fer a good seeing to – when you woke me up.'

'Tough luck is that Roy, especially as in your dreams is the only place that you'll be walking out with a beautiful blonde.'

'Ar'll not tell yer again ye two!' bellowed nana. 'Get down here now! Yer cornflakes are going soft!'

'No change there then,' muttered Roy. 'Why they canna leave them in the cereal box an' let us see to our own, is beyond me.'

Alistair dived into the bathroom and swilled his face with water before dashing back into the bedroom to dress in haste.

Roy was out of bed and getting dressed – not bothering with a morning wash. Still half awake, he yawned loudly, stretching himself and letting out a big fart in the process. 'Bah! That's better.'

'Yer've not shit yer sen have yer?'

'No, that was a dry 'en thank God.'

'I've just had a thought our Roy . . . It's Friday today.'

'That's very perceptive of you. Have you been reading them encyclopedias again?'

'No, listen . . . keep quiet.'

'I canna hear a thing.'

'Exactly. I've not heard that sawmill all week.'

'Aye, an' yer winna hear it next week an' all. Donny's away to Blackpool fer a fortnight – ar heard Lottie telling me mother he was ganning away last Saturday.'

Steady on, yer daft pair o' buggers,' scolded Roy's mother, Alistair's auntie Kitty. 'Yer'll break yer necks ganning at that speed.'

The boys seated themselves at the dining table and got stuck in to their cornflakes, while auntie Kitty sat by the open fire toasting some bread which would soon be smothered in treacle.

'That baking smells nice,' commented Alistair.

'Ar's doing some pies and buns fer tomorrows trip hinny,' explained nana.

The following day, the women and children would all be going on the annual Stanhope Working Mens Club day trip to Whitley Bay.

Roy had protested on more than one occasion that he was too old for a kids day out at the seaside, but to no avail. His mother had pointed out that they never went anywhere together and Roy's objections proved futile. Every time he gave thought to the outing, it filled him with horror. He visualised himself sitting on the bus . . . All those noisy kids farting with excitement, especially when the coach neared the coastline. 'Look mammy, ar can see the sea!' plop, plop. They're underpants were probably encrusted with shite. Some of the grandmothers were nee better. They smelled of what he could only describe as a mixture of mothballs and piss. If it was a hot day – and you can bet your bottom dollar it would be – the coach would be like a travelling furnace, stinking to high heaven. Still, there'd be a couple of crates of lukewarm, past its best pop, stacked at the rear of the coach, along with a tin of soggy crisps. One bag per child mind, and don't forget to bring the empty bottles back – there's a penny on every hundred returned. All this wonderful fare generously donated by the working mens club committee. Tight as Lionel Blairs arse cheeks, them buggers.

No, I think you could safely say without fear of contradiction, that this day trip to Whitley Bay would not go down as the highlight of Roy's young life.

'How come me granda doesn't 'ave to gan on this stupid day trip?' he complained.

'Simple bonny lad,' explained nana. 'It's women and children only. You already nar that though, divent yer? Yer've been ganning fer the last ten years.'

'Aye, how can ar forget? Ar deserve a bloody long service medal.'

'Language Roy!'

'Sorry mother – But ar can see me sen still 'aving to gan when ar's eighteen.'

'Stop exaggerating. Ar've telt yer before, that next year yer can please yer sen whether yer gan on it or not.'

'Can I have that in writing?'

'Yer've got my word – that's enough.'

'Well I'm going to enjoy this trip,' enthused Alistair. 'Especially if the weather's like this.'

'Aye, you'll be able to mek sandcastles with your bucket an' spade an' stick a little flag in 'em,' sneered Roy.

'Whey, at least our Alistair's got the right attitude in going with the intention of enjoying him sen,' rebuked nana. 'You've written the day off before it's begun, yer miserable so and so.'

'He's at that funny age mother,' sighed Kitty, trying to make excuses for him. 'He should grow out of it soon. Another month an' he'll be fifteen.'

Roy resented this chatter about him between his nana and his mother. It was as if they were oblivious to him being there. Still, he kept his thoughts and feelings to himself.

'Ar divent nar what plans ye two have fer today,' said Kitty. 'But before yer gan gallavanting off anywhere, yer can nip down the co-op for us. There's a shopping list on the table.'

'Aye, okay mother. After that, me an' our Alistair are off rose hipping – Earn some brass fer Stanhope Show weekend. It'll be here afore yer know it.'

The annual Stanhope Agricultural Show was the villagers

highlight of the year. That – and the odd bit of cock fighting was their only excitement.

Roy had told Alistair that he was going to enter the previous cock fight, claiming that with his big John Thomas, he was bound to win.

Alistair had to explain to the moron that it was not that type of cock fight, but the feathered kind. Well . . . they started out with feathers, but the fighting birds would soon strip each other down to their birthday suits. Not a pretty sight, but at least you could crow about it. Unlike the poor defeated cock, whose voice box had been ripped out, and left amongst the other entrails.

The boys had never been to one of these fights, and probably never would, as they were just stories spread about by the older boys trying to act big.

This time of year was just right to go rose hipping. The hips would be nice and full – perfect for picking.
The boys went hipping every year, filling their haversacks to bursting with the bright red berries before taking them to a building within the castle grounds near the market place. There, they would be weighed and exchanged for money.

Roy was not averse to adding some soil to his bag, just to add that extra bit of weight, hence – more brass. He got away with it because the bags were weighed still strapped up. You yourself emptied the hips afterwards into a large wooden box. Rummaging your hands in the box, the soil just disappeared – no one any the wiser.

He didn't miss a trick didn't Roy, but Alistair wouldn't follow his example, telling him that it was dishonest. This irritated Roy somewhat – thinking what a socialist little prick he was. He should be an enterprising capitalist like himself. The fact that Alistair had informed Roy he wasn't a capitalist but just a con man, cut no ice with him. Wait until he were a few years older – he'd soon get him thinking his way. A period of time spent with the master would soon shake the goody two shoes out of him.

'Ha way Ali, the co-op it is. Ar've got this shipping order, you grab the shopping bag,' ordered Roy, before muttering under his breath, 'It suits yer, yer little puff.'

'What was that?'

'Nowt, ar was just saying – ar was out of puff. Must be a bit of hay fever or summat.'

'Morning Mrs Lister,' acknowledged Roy of his neighbour, who was standing on her doorstep as usual.

'Aye,' came the reply, which for her was a substantial statement.

'Have you seen the face on her our Ali? It's like a bulldog licking piss off a nettle. Ar bet the last time she smiled, she pulled a face muscle.'

'She's not doing any harm to anybody,' said Alistair, defending her. 'She's probably lonely.'

'Whey, she is married yer nar, but he works away a lot the lucky bugger. He's not daft eh? She must 'ave some money or summat – he can't 'ave married her for her looks. Still . . . yer don't look at the fireplace when yer poking the fire, do yer bonny lad?'

'If people knew what you said about them, they'd have a fit.'

'What they divent nar canna harm them. Dinna sweat man.'

Turning left at the bottom of the Square bank, Alistair noticed three of the old boys sitting on the benches at the bottom of Paragon Street. 'Oh no,' he groaned. 'We won't get back home until tea-time if you start stirring the old fellows up.'

'Two minutes chat, just to be polite like.'

'You? Polite? Don't make me laugh.'

'Morning gentlemen. I use the term loosely mind,' baited Roy.

Old Tom took it – he never could resist. 'Whey, what d'yer mean – use the term loosely? Before you here, are three of Stanhopes finest citizens, past and present.'

Alistair sat himself down, resigned to being here for the duration.

'You should look up to your your elders,' chided Tom.

'Ar'd 'ave a job on – Ye old buggers are always sat down.'

'Yer nar what ar mean young Osborne. Yer should learn some

respect. It wouldn't harm yer to polish our boots – when yer passing like,' said Tom, winking at his companions, Fred Brown and Ronnie Doyle.

'Whey, why should yer need yer boots polishing? Yer never tek 'em any where apart from the pub – an' it's not muddy in there is it? Oh sorry, ar forgot – yer gan to the post office once a week for yer free cash hand out. Ar think ye lot call it beer money, if ar's not mistaken.'

'Hand out my backside!' objected Tom. 'We've earned it – Fought in two world wars so's the likes of ye can walk the streets freely in a democratic society.'

'That's not the tale ar heard,' scoffed Roy, feeling smug with himself for getting Tom going again. 'They say yer went missing both wars, turning up again when they were over. Rumour has it that yer were a coward – but that's not fer me to say.'

'Gan away an' shite, yer little bugger! Ar's the most decorated war hero Stanhope's ever had.'

'Whey, Fred there telt me that you bought them medals that you're always flashing round. Yer bought 'em at a Durham indoor market stall fer a couple o' bob.'

'Ar never said owt o' the sort,' protested Fred. 'Divent listen to a word he says Tom. You're asking fer a kick up the backside lad.'

'He's got ye ganning now Fred lad!' chuckled Ronnie. 'An' that teks some deeing! You're quiet young Alistair, not like yer cousin.'

'Well I can't get a word in. He's like this all the time Mr Doyle. I just switch off. If I didn't, I'd end up in the looney bin.'

'Ha way our kid,' proclaimed Roy. 'We'd better get the shopping done, or they'll be 'aving kittens back home.'

'Aye, an' we'd better get ganning as well,' stated Fred. 'Check on them prize leeks o' yours Tom. Pub'll be open soon, so get thee skates on.'

'Prize leeks my arse,' scoffed Roy. 'Yer might as well bin 'em now. Yer'll never beat me granda's. Yer just wasting yer time man.'

'We'll see,' said Tom struggling to his feet. 'It's not long to

Stanhope Show now. Anyway . . . we're off. Cheerio lads.'

'See yer. Come on Ali, we'll be getting shot.'

The co-op was fairly quiet as the lads walked in. There were just a few local women in, doing more gossiping than shopping.

It didn't take long for Roy's mouth to get back into gear. 'Hey up Jim – How's yer belly fer spots?'

'Oh no,' groaned Jim. 'Just when ar thought ar was in for a nice quiet morning.'

'Whey, we are quiet aren't we Alistair? As long as you divent keep us waiting all day like. This shopping list is urgent – Molly an' me mother are dying of starvation.'

'Whey, get thee pipe, I'm serving these charming young ladies at the moment.'

'Bah, yer a smooth talker you Jim Morrison,' said Mrs Green sarcastically. 'Does your Betty know how yer flirt with yer female customers?'

'Don't flatter yer sen Mrs,' interrupted Roy. 'He's just the same with the men. Excuse me madam,' he said scratching his head. 'Ar's sure I know you – Ar just canna **plaice** you. No – wait, ar tell a lie. You're that fish an' chip shop man's wife – Mrs Green, if I'm not mistaken.'

'Very funny Roy,' said Mrs Green. 'Still the same, shy retiring type I see.' She turned to Alistair. 'How are you Alistair? I don't really have to ask do I? I know you love it up here.'

'I certainly do Mrs Green. We're off on the club trip to Whitley Bay tomorrow,' he informed her excitedly.

'Whey, ar hope the weather stays fine for you all. It's a canny forecast for the weekend like.'

'You're not tekking your Roy with yer are yer?' inquired Mrs Swales.

'I'm afraid so. With a bit of luck we might be allowed to stick him in the coach boot.'

'Whey, ar divent even want to go on this stupid kids trip anyway,' objected Roy. Ar'll be fifteen in a couple of weeks fer petes sake. Me mother thinks ar's still a ten year old.'

'You still act like a ten year old,' muttered Jim.

'Yer won't be saying that Mr Morrison when ar become Stanhopes youngest ever MP. Ar'll have the health inspector calling on yer. He'll 'ave yer shut down in nee time – state o' this place.'

'Arraway with yer – This place is spotless.'

'I'm sorry Jim . . . It's got to be said, and ar derive nee pleasure in divulging the local rumours with regards as to how filthy your shop really is. In fact, they say it's so dirty, even the mice wear overalls.'

'Yer daft bugger. Excuse the language ladies,' apologised Jim. 'But he'd mek a parson swear, young Osborne.'

'There was a fight last week in your fish an' chip shop Mrs Green,' announced Roy.

'Oh really?' she replied, trying to sound suitably shocked. 'It must 'ave been when ar wasn't there then. What happened like?'

'Two fish got battered,' chuckled Roy.

'Eeh, yer get worse Roy lad.'

'How come we hardly ever see you in the fish shop Mrs Green? Does your Harold keep you in the back, peeling tatties an' skinning the fish while he chats up the birds ower the front counter?'

'What? That frigid fish fryer? An' that's not his nickname fer nowt, yer nar . . . No, if the truth be known, I like working in the back of the shop where it's quieter. Ar prefer to leave all the noisy customers like yerself, to our Harold. He's very placid yer see . . . Sometimes ar have to shake him to see if he's still alive, he's that laid back.'

'Well, I must say that your fish and chips are very nice,' complimented Alistair. 'Very tasty.'

'Thank you very much – that's nice to hear. It meks a change from all the professional moaners,' she said, nodding in the direction of Roy.

Roy was thinking to himself, what a creeping little prick Alistair was, and that he was probably after getting bigger portions.

'Fair do's – ar must admit of late, I have noticed a slight improvement in your product . . . The batter's nice an' crispy, and the fish a little tastier. In fact . . . Harold's getting a **dab** hand at frying. Ar still think he's a **shark** though, the prices he charges. Last week, he gave me a fish wi' long whiskers sticking out. When ar complained, he told me to stop moaning – said it were a **cat** fish.'

'Very good Roy,' groaned Alistair. 'Me sides are aching with laughing so much.'

'Misery guts . . . Ar bet ye divent gan to Whitley Bay fer your holidays Mrs Green. The money Harold teks off us, yer'll be able to gan ower the watter to Costa Bravo.'

'Chance'd be a fine thing . . . He's not known fer throwing his money around isn't our Harold.'

'Whey, we all nar him as Scrooge – No offence intended Mrs Green,' apologised Roy, somewhat unconvincingly.

'None tekken lad, divent worry. Ar can understand how they come to give him that nickname. Eeh . . . The last time we went on holiday, rationing was still on. Do yer nar . . . ? On the rare occasions we go fer a drink together, we have to stay in the club all night because the drinks are cheaper there than in the pub. Aye . . . Harold'll be the richest man in the graveyard. Anyway — It's been nice talking to yer, but ar'll have to get ganning – we'll be opening up the shop soon. Give my best up the Square. Bye Jim.'

'Cheerio Mrs Green, Mrs Swales.'

'Aye, cheerio,' echoed the lads.

'Stick a crate o' beer on that shopping list Jim. Ar'll tek it wi' me to Whitley Bay.'

'Certainly Roy – in another three years when it's legal.'

'Spoilsport. Ar need summat to get me through tomorrow, when ar's stuck on a bus full of screaming, farting, over excited kids . . . An' that's just our Alistair.'

'At least I won't be sat sulking like a big baby. I'm going to make the most of it.'

'That's the spirit Alistair lad. If moaning minnie there, gets yer down, a few of yer want to get together an' bury the bugger on the beach – do us all a favour.'

'Divent tell lies, yer'd miss me man. This poor excuse fer a shop would be even duller than it is now, without my magnetic personality. Stick the price o' two frozen Jubblys down on that list an' mek 'em disappear in wi' the general shopping will yer? Nana an' me mother winna know the difference.'

Jim was weighing out sugar into a blue bag. 'It's a tale. Ar divent want them two reigning down on me. Ar'd rather wrestle wi' Billy Two Rivers. Get yer sens one each, ar'll treat yer – just this once mind.'

'Cheers Jim. Yer not as bad as they all mek yer out to be, after all. Ar've always stood up fer yer against the local gossips.'

'Yes, yes Roy . . . Just get the Jubblys an' stop yer arse licking. Alistair . . . Pass me a packet o' tea will yer please?' Jim weighed out the butter and wrapped it in greaseproof paper. 'And a bottle of Tizer,' he muttered to himself, reaching under the counter.

Roy was wandering round the shop, examining the merchandise on display looking for fault. 'Urgh! There's a load o' flies in these breadcakes!' he exclaimed.

'They're currants, yer daft bat!' admonished Jim. 'Stop messsing an' pass me one of them tins o' beans an' sausages straight in front of yer.' The shop doorbell rang. 'Good morning Mrs Burns, how are you on this fine morning? Well I trust, and your Frank?'

'We're both fine, thank you Jim. Our Frank's round his allotment, nursing his vegetables ready fer the show. Ar don't know why he bothers – he never wins anything. Ar think it's just an excuse to sit in his shed with his hip flask, reading the Racing Post. How's yerself anyway?'

'Can't complain – but ar winna be sorry when one o'clock comes round an' I can tek a break. My assistant, Janet should be back by then. She was ganning to the hospital with her mother this morning.'

'Whey, where's your Betty then?'

'Gone to Bishop, visiting her mother, but if I nar her – she'll be spending my money as well, no doubt.'

'Whey, yer must have plenty,' said Roy butting in. 'The prices ye charge in here.'

'Oh, yer still awake ar see. It must be a full two minutes since you were chelping on. Ar divent set the prices bonny lad, the Co-operative Society see to that. Mrs Morrison an' my good self just get a wage. We don't get any extra payment fer putting up wi' the likes of ye either. Here we are, ar've finished yer order,' he announced, putting the last item into the shopping bag. 'That'll be nine shillings and sixpence fer cash please.'

Roy handed him a ten shilling note.

'Thank you,' said Jim, giving Roy his change. 'Give my best to everyone up the Square won't you?'

'Aye, will do. Here yer are Alistair – You tek the shopping bag an' ar'll carry the bottle o' Tizer.'

'Don't you strain yer sen will yer?' carped Alistair. 'I'm not a donkey you know.'

'Ar nar that bonny lad, but I am . . . according to all the local lasses.'

Jim coughed loudly.

'Oh, sorry Mrs Burns,' apologised Roy. 'Ar hope ar didn't offend you.'

'That's alright, ar didn't hear you,' she said diplomatically.

The boys set off home, bumping into Billy shortly after leaving the shop.

'Alright lads, how yer ganning?'

'We'll be champion, once we've dropped this shopping off. We can gan an' get some brass earned then, rose hipping. Do yer fancy coming along like?' asked Roy.

'Nar, ar's away to Crook today to visit our Eddie.'

'Are you going on the trip to Whitley Bay tomorrow Billy?' asked Alistair.

'Whey aye, bonny lad. All them gorgeous birds at the Spanish City amusement park'll be expecting me.'

'Erm . . . ar divent think so Sonny Jim,' intervened Roy. 'Have yer forgot that the Stanhope Stud will be making an appearance?'

'Nar – Ar've already said, ar's ganning,' confirmed Billy.

'Not you, yer prat – **me**!'

'Blooming heck!' exclaimed Alistair. 'You've changed yer tune 'aven't yer? This morning you were pleading with me auntie Kitty not to mek yer go on the trip. How come yer've changed yer mind?'

'Ar may have been a little hasty in not wanting to gan. Last year was a wash out, if yer remember. It poured down all day – kept all the birds at home. The forecast looks canny fer tomorrow, hence – there'll be loads of lasses hanging aboot the amusement park, just waiting fer the Stanhope Stud to turn up. Ye two stick with me tomorrow, an' watch an' learn. The master will be on the prowl . . . So lock up your daughters Whitley Bay, Errol flynn is on his way!'

'More like Vera Lynn is on his way,' scoffed Alistair. 'I can just see him tomorrow, standing by the waltzers chewing gum, trying to look cool with his hedgehog haircut, wearing his winkle pickers. All the lasses'll be taking the mickey out of him, but he's that thick skinned, he won't know.'

'Ye may mock Yorky boy, but at least ar winna be paddling in the sea, holding me nana an' aunties hand.'

'Well that's where yer wrong clever clogs, 'cause I'm going to the Spanish City too – I'm old enough this year. Me nana and auntie Kitty are going to play bingo, so they said I can go along with you.'

'Whey, yer can tag along with me, nee problem,' proclaimed Roy. 'Just divent get jealous when ar's surrounded by gorgeous birds, because yer bound to feel inadequate, it's only natural.'

'The only birds hanging round you'll be a flock o' seagulls,' mocked Billy. 'With a bit o' luck, they might shite on yer, an' then yer'll be walking round wi' flies buzzing round yer heed.'

The boys had just stopped outside the police station when Stanhope's constable PC Fowler came out of the front door. He lived just around the corner in Paragon Street. You couldn't miss his house, there was a blue lantern on the front wall with the word POLICE printed on it in bold lettering.

'Hello, hello, hello, what do we have here then? Three local scallywags, loitering with intent – one with a dubious haircut. Have you got a licence for that barnet Mr Osborne?'

'Very funny, PC Fowler,' said Roy with a sarcastic laugh. 'Are yer ganning on yer daily street patrol then?'

'That's right son. I shall proceed to patrol the main street, my presence as usual giving reassurance to the natives of Stanhope.

Safe in the knowledge that they can go about their daily business undisturbed and be able to sleep soundly in their beds at night, knowing that PC Fowler is on the beat.'

'You must be very busy,' said Roy. 'Do yer find the time to tek a lunch break, what – with your heavy work schedule an' all?

'Not really. I'm not one for taking much of a break anyway. You see, I'm a very conscientious worker. I usually just grab a sandwich from Bon Bon's.'

'What do yer get to eat? A truncheon meat sandwich?'

'It's not like you to be funny Roy, and once again, you don't disappoint.'

'Shouldn't you arrest him fer jokes like that constable?' questioned Alistair.

'You're probably right young 'en, but I ask you – Would you like to be confined to the same building as him? He'd drive me round the bend.'

'Is it true that prisoners only get dry bread an' watter?' asked Billy.

'No, they get proper meals an' are well looked after.'

'Do you 'ave to cook their meals an' serve 'em then?'

'No,' he stated. 'It's very rare anyone's detained in our cells. If they are, it's usually just overnight. Next morning they're shipped off to Durham prison. I might make them the odd sandwich and a cuppa, but as I say, it's very rare anybody's detained here. Right, I think it's time I did the rounds. What are you lot up to today?' The policeman's natural inquisitiveness coming to the fore. (Some might call it being nosey.)

'Whey, me an' our Alistair's ganning rose hipping – get a few bob fer the show like. Billy's off to their kids in Crook.'

'Well, behave yerselves an' keep off them railway lines won't yer? I don't want to hear of anyone being crushed to death fer the sake of a few rosehips.'

The constables concern was not unfounded. Many bushes grew by the fencing along the railway, and in the not too distant past, one or two lads had been involved in some near misses.

'We'll be very careful PC Fowler,' Roy reassured him. 'An' ar'll mek sure ar have some reins on our Alistair.' He couldn't resist injecting some wit, even into a serious conversation.

'Just take care lads. I'll see you all later.'

'Aye, cheerio constable. Have a good day,' said Roy, creeping as usual.

PC Fowler set off on his beat down the main street.

'Ar's off as well,' announced Billy, 'Or ar'll miss me bus. See yer in Jo Jo's tonight, seven to half past.'

'Aye, alright, see yer tonight.'

'Cheerio Billy,' added Alistair.

'Blooming heck, yer here at last!' exclaimed Kitty. We were just ganna send out a search party to look for yer, weren't we mother?'

'Aye lass, we were. I was beginning to think they'd moved the co-op to Frosterley.'

Frosterley was the next village on. It lay between Stanhope and Wolsingham, which was six miles away.

'Whey, it's not our fault,' protested Roy. 'Jim Morrison was left to run the co-op on his own. Apparently, his assistant Janet didn't turn up. Ar think she'd gone to the hospital with her mother – summat like that.'

'Whey, wasn't Betty Morrison working?' inquired Kitty.

'No mother. Jim said she'd gone to Bishop to spend his hard earned money.'

'It's ganning to pot lately, that co-op. The service is poor an' yer canna get half the things yer want. Whey, ar maybe exaggerating there a bit, but there's usually a couple of things on yer list that yer come home without. If they got their orders in earlier with the suppliers, it would be nee problem.'

'Whey, it sounds to me we'd all be better off with you managing the place our Kitty,' commented nana.

'Ar'd make a better fist of it, that's fer sure. Did you manage to get everything on the list our Roy?'

'Aye as it 'appened, here's the change.'

'Pass me the tin of beans an' sausages hinny,' said nana. 'Ar'll dee yer a spot o' lunch before yer gan off rose hipping fer the afternoon.'

'Here you are nana,' obliged Alistair, taking the tin into the kitchen.

'Thanks pet. Ar've made up a bottle of diluted orange juice to tek with yer. Get the haversacks out of the cubby hole, then sit yer sens down at the table.'

The cubby hole was a store room directly under the stairs and was adjacent to the dining room fire. Grandad kept his boot polish and brushes in there.

As Alistair took out the haversacks, he noticed two piles of Beano comics at the back of the cupboard. 'Do you save all yer old Beanos Roy?' he asked.

'Aye,' came Roy's reply. 'An' there's another stack in the coal shed as well,' he declared proudly. 'Don't ask why – ar just like keeping things. Ar's a bit of a magpie really, hoarding things. Me mother thinks ar should bin 'em or give 'em to a jumble sale. Says they take up too much space.'

'Well don't throw them away, whatever you do. If you decide to get rid of 'em, I'll take 'em back to Leeds with me. Whatever you do, don't bin them – it'd be such a waste.'

'Whey, ar'll keep it in mind bonny lad.'

The boys seated themselves at the dining room table. Nana and auntie Kitty came through from the kitchen, each carrying a plate.

'Beans and sausages on toast,' announced nana. 'This should keep yer ganning until tea-time.'

'Thanks nana,' said Alistair, tucking in eagerly. 'I love the taste of these sausages. Aren't you two having any?'

'No bonny lad. Kitty an' me are having a boiled egg each, aren't we **chuck**?'

'That was a **poultry** joke nana. In fact, it was **fowl**.'

'You can't resist can yer Roy?' groaned Alistair.

'Whey, ar divent like to **chicken** out like. When ar went past the Grey Bull the other week, there was a rake of chickens drinking beer out of a large dish. Aye, it were a **hen** party.'

'Oh, dear,' chuckled his mother. 'Now eat yer dinner afore it gans cold.'

After lunch, the boys were given orders to take Lassie for a quick run on the back field. Lassie was kept in the shed come coal house. While Roy was in there, he sorted out two pairs of canvas gloves. Grandad had brought home several pairs from his job on the bin wagon. They came in handy for a wide range of jobs and were ideal for rose hipping. The stems supporting the red hips were very prickly. Wearing gloves to pluck them was the sensible option.

After ten minutes, the lads were coming back down the side of the house and returning Lassie to her kennel.
 Alistair took the dogs drinking bowl into the kitchen for some fresh water.
 'Bah, that was quick. Did Lassie 'ave time to yawn?' teased nana.
 'She's panting actually,' replied Alistair. 'I know we weren't long, but once in the field – you'd think our Lassie were a greyhound.'
 'Ar's only kidding pet. Ar nar she gets plenty of exercise. Yer granda teks her round yon field every morning afore he gans to work.'
 Roy came in from the yard. 'Ha way with that watter our kid, it's time we weren't here. There's loads of big juicy red hips, just waiting to be gathered up an' turned into brass fer our pockets.'
 Alistair nipped back into the yard and put the water down for Lassie. 'There yer are girl, have a nice drink,' he said patting her fondly. Closing the back yard gate behind him, he shot into the house. 'Right, I'm ready,' he announced.
 'Tek an 'aversack then,' ordered Roy. 'There's a pair of gloves in each one. Oh . . . an' I put the orange juice in yours.'
 'Surprise, surprise. That's very generous of you Roy, letting me have the honour of being pop carrier fer the day. I mustn't forget to return the gesture someday.'
 'Never mind the sarcasm . . . Just grab yer 'aversack an' let's get ganning – time's money. See yer later mother, nana.'
 'Aye okay lads,' said Kitty.
 'Be careful mind,' added nana. 'Nee ganning on the railway tracks, or owt daft like that.'
 'Yes . . . Divent worry. We've already had a lecture this morning

aboot the dangers of the railway. PC Fowler got on his soapbox and proceded to instill in us the perils of laying across the railway lines, especially when a train is approaching. Said it wasn't much of a life when you were decapitated . . . apart from being famous fer a short time the next day when you made the headlines in the Northern Echo.'

'By, that was nearly funny,' scoffed Alistair. 'You're ahead of your time.'

'Hey, divent ye start, we've enough with that daft bugger!' chortled auntie Kitty. 'Now, get yer sens off, the day's nearly ower with. Back by half four mind.'

The boys set off down the Square.

'Whey, that's odd . . . There's nee Mrs Lister on the front doorstep. Ar wonder if she's kicked the bucket, or is that just wishful thinking?' sniggered Roy.

'Don't be so rotten,' objected Alistair. 'She might be having forty winks – catching up on some beauty sleep.'

'Beauty sleep?' exclaimed Roy, incredulously. 'The old bat will be asleep fer at least twenty years then!'

'Eeh . . . the stuff you come out with.'

'Many a true word spoken in jest bonny lad.'

Out of the corner of his eye, Roy was aware of Mr Hardcastle on his doorstep. A few weeks earlier, Alistair had been walking down the street and in passing, had been looking at his reflection in the window of the house that unfortunately belonged to Mr Hardcastle. He had immediately shouted at Alistair, 'Had a good look lad!' This had upset Alistair somewhat, but Roy had consoled him by telling him not to take any notice of Hardcastle, who happened to be a prat and a cantankerous swine who didn't work – preferring to sit at home all day drinking bottles of beer, while his wife was out earning the money.

'Hold yer breath our kid,' Roy warned Alistair as they approached Hardcastle. 'If he breathes on you, it'll knock you ower. He could fire a jet engine with that breath.'

The boys walked past him not making eye contact, thus giving no cause to pick an argument.

'Did yer get a whiff of 'im our Alistair?'

'Not 'alf . . . An' I was giving him a wide berth. It's a good job you didn't 'ave a cigarette in yer gob – we'd 'ave been blown on to the rooftops. It's a wonder he hasn't already blown himself up anyway. You hardly ever see him without a fag hanging from his miserable mouth.'

'Whey he wouldn't feel it either,' added Roy. 'He'd be that numb wi' the booze.'

Chapter 2

The boys reached the stepping stones which crossed over the river Wear.
Roy went to the waters edge and searched amongst the pebbles there. Selecting the smoothest, flattest ones, he started skimming them over the ford adjacent to the stepping stones.
'I thought you were in a hurry to get some brass earned,' remarked Alistair.
'Get thee pipe man, ar's coming. You set off ower the steppys an' ar'll catch yer up in a minute.'
There wasn't anyone coming from the opposite direction, so Alistair set off.
Having crossed the stepping stones on countless occasions, the boys were very adept at it.
Having taken a dozen steps there was a splash, followed by a huge spray of water. Alistair instinctively knew where the source of his soaking came from and looked round to see Roy at the rivers edge bent double, laughing his socks off.
'You're mental, you are!' he shouted. 'I should 'ave known you were up to summat when yer told me to go on ahead. I'll get you back – don't worry about that!'
'Ar's sorry kidder.'
'You liar! You're wallowing in it!'
'Correction . . . Ar think yer mean **you're** wallowing in it bonny lad! Ar just couldn't resist,' he chuckled, making his way towards Alistair, trying his best to keep a straight face.
'Your day will come, you mark my words.'

'That sounds a bit dramatic. What yer ganna dee? Murder me in me sleep like? It was only a splash of watter fer petes sake.'
'Only a splash of water? I'm soaked to the skin!'
'Stop exaggerating man.'
'It's alright for you, you're not the one who'll be laid up in bed tomorrow with pneumonia. If I only had a splash of water on me, how come I'm covered in moss?'
'Steady on cracking the funnys, that's my job. Ha way, let's get some hip picking done. You'll soon dry out this weather.'

They walked a short distance up the road, Alistair still sulking. He wasn't half as wet as he made out, he was just taking a leaf out of Roy's book – the great pretender that he was. This course of action worried him somewhat. The thought that there was the remotest chance he might be turning into anything resembling Roy, filled him with horror.

'There's some big juicy hips over there,' noticed Roy. 'Come on, let's gan ower here.'

They climbed over a stone wall and proceded towards a wooden fence next to the railway track. Rosehip bushes grew next to the fence, clinging and inter-weaving between the wooden slats.

'Right boy, these are begging to be plucked by uncle Roy. Ar winna disappoint 'em. Divent forget to put yer gloves on bonny lad – we don't want yer getting prickled, all that water'll pour out of yer an' leave yer dehydrated.'

'Just get on with yer hipping,' grumbled Alistair. 'Give the verbals a rest will you?'

'Ooh, touchy. Keep yer 'air on son – Yer wet hair that is. Ar divent want us to **drift** apart.'

'That's it! – I'm off to the next bush,' announced Alistair.

Putting some ten yards distance between him and Roy, Alistair dropped his haversack and delved into his pocket. He pulled out some toilet paper. Screwing some up into two small balls, he put one in each ear. He then got to work, doing what he came here for, picking rosehips.

Roy looked on, shaking his head from side to side, a wry smile on his face. 'Please yer sen, yer big babby!' he shouted, then

added, 'Yer big water babby!'
 'Bollocks!'
 'Yer'll 'ave a pair, when yer a man!'

An hour had gone by and the boys haversacks were almost full with the bright red hips.
 The sound of a train in the distance turned their heads.
 'Aren't yer ganna lie across the rails an' top yerself our Alistair?' goaded Roy.
 'No, an' I won't let you get to me either. You flatter yerself too much.'
 'Whey, if yer not ower offended with me, would yer pass that orange ower here then? Ar's dying o' thirst.'
 'Here,' said Alistair grudgingly, walking over and handing him the pop. 'I hope it chokes you,' he added without much conviction, his annoyance with Roy having subsided. He couldn't hold a grudge for too long.
 'Are yer talking to me now then?' asked Roy.
 'Might be.'
 'Ar'll tek that as a yes then,' said Roy, somewhat relieved. 'Have yer nearly filled yer 'aversack?'
 'Yeah, another couple o' dozen an' it'll be full.'
 'Me too.'
 'Is that with or without soil in the bottom?' scoffed Alistair.
 'Without. Ar like to give 'em full value fer money with my first donation. It's a sort of tradition with me.'
 'Bah, you're all heart Roy. Remind me to put yer name forward for Stanhope's citizen of the year award.'
 The train passed them, taking ages to tail off with what seemed like an endless stream of empty wagons coupled on to the engine. The train was making its way to Eastgate a few miles up the track, to the newly opened cement works there.
 'Ar've just had a brilliant idea our Alistair, but it involves your assistance.'
 'Oh no . . . ' Alistair groaned. 'What now – dare I ask?'
 'Whey, just bear with me and my cunning plot shall be revealed. Yer nar the cement train? Course yer do – one's just passed us,

daft question.'

'Don't tell me,' said Alistair, 'When the next train comes down the track, you're gonna hijack it an' take it to Bishop Auckland, give all the girls there a good seeing to an' then return home, just in time fer tea.'

'Bloody hell Alistair, that's exactly what I'm ganna do!' Did yer read me mind – Yer not psychopathic are yer?'

'You mean a psychic.'

'You're the one that's psychotic. Whatever . . . Anyway, ar've nothing so drastic up me sleeve, but cement is summat to do with it . . . First things first though. I want ye to nip home an' sneak a shovel out of the coal shed. Keep yer heed down when yer passing the kitchen window mind. Divent stop to groom Lassie either Doctor Doolittle. Grab a spade an' one o' me granda's empty sacks, an' then get yer sen back here sharpish like.'

'Is that all I've got to do? You wouldn't prefer me to steal a JCB an' a dumper truck instead?'

'Now yer talking daft.'

'I'm talking daft? That's a bit rich coming from you. Tell me, do, what this cunning plan of yours entails. Go on, surprise me.'

'Okay, this is what 'appens . . . After you've got the equipment, we lay in wait fer the next full cement train to come down the track.'

'Before you ask . . . I'm not lying across the rails to stop the train.'

'You divent have to, you silly lad! retorted Roy. 'You've seen how they chug along at a snails pace 'aven't yer?'

'Go on.'

'Whey, ar'll climb on the fence an' bide me time, then jump onto one of the rear wagons . . . This is where you come in useful.'

'That must be a first . . . Just get on with it windbag.'

'Right – you'll chuck me the shovel, then you'll run alongside of the train with the open sack. Ar'll shovel cement into it an' then leap off. Nee one'll see us. The engine driver doesn't 'ave wing mirrors, an' even if by chance he looks back an' spies us, he's hardly ganna pull up an' chase after us. The wagon trains are that long, if he shouted at us, we wouldn't hear him. He'd need a megaphone.'

'What do you want cement for anyway?'

'Whey, a couple o' handfuls mixed in with the rosehips an' it sticks yer earning potential right up.'

'Don't you think it's a bit over the top going to such lengths for a few shovels of cement? Do you walk about with yer eyes closed or summat? Because I've noticed that on the track where there are connecting joints, cement's fallen off the wagons. I'd 'ave thought it more practical to go an' scoop that lot into the sack instead.' Alistair knew that Roy was bullshitting, but by playing along, acting serious, Roy's attempts at humour had backfired on himself.

'What ar said aboot getting a shovel an' jumping on the cement wagon . . . ar was only kidding yer nar.'

Alistair put on a surprised look. 'Never! An' there was me, thinking what a great mastermind I was in the presence of.'

'Ha ha, yer sarky sod. Yer nar your trouble divent yer? Nee sense o' humour.'

'Well yer wrong there, because I do have a sense of humour – I just haven't heard anything funny. Come on, get yer haversack an' let's get weighed in.'

They strolled beside the river, making their way to the castle grounds in the market place. They crossed over a bridge adjacent to Stanhope show field. The bridge had originally been a swing bridge and was still known by that name. It was now a cast iron construction with a wooden boarded floor.

In the past, the boys would haul up boulders from below and drop them over the parapet, enjoying the loud splashing noise they made as they hit the river. The cascading fountain of water would reach high into the air, showering the lads. This was welcomed on hot sunny days.

Halfway across the bridge, Alistair spotted some people sitting on a bench beneath the castle's high perimeter wall. The characters were well known to him, as most of the natives were. Alistair steeled himself in preparation for another long delay –

The forthcoming bullshit was inevitable. Actually, if the truth be known, he enjoyed 'the crack' – and whose football team was the best, would always enter into the conversation.

Frank Noland, a native of Stanhope was sitting with Don and Olga Shand, a couple of 'townies' who had moved to Stanhope after retiring. The couple were from Sunderland, but to be fair, it wasn't their fault.

Roy always insisted they'd been exiled for unsociable behaviour. Don and Olga fervently denied this allegation, insisting that after a life of hard work and toil, they'd moved to Stanhope to enjoy their autumn years in the beautiful village.

Locals weren't too keen on 'townies' moving into their territory, occupying properties intended for the habitation of the natives of Stanhope. Some of them would walk past Don and Olga pretending not to notice them, but Don would always pass the time of day, asking how they were, or what a grand day it was. Even though he was known as the local bore, folks gave in to him in the end by giving him the cursory 'aye'. That's if they hadn't already seen him coming, and had had the chance to cross the road to avoid him. Don was a thick skinned bugger though, and it was like water off a ducks back to him.

'Nar then ye two buggers, what's in them haversacks?' quizzed Frank. 'Yer've not filled 'em with pebbles 'ave yer, to pass off as rosehips?'

'Eeh . . . As if we would do owt like that,' retorted Roy. 'Shame on yer Frank.'

'There's not my brass candlesticks in there I hope?' teased Don.

'Whey, isn't that typical of a macam our Alistair? Coming up here, casting aspersions on our integrity.'

'Bloody hell!' exclaimed Don. "Ave you eaten a dictionary fer breakfast?'

'Nar, I think they call it intelligence, but ar'll talk simpler ter yer if it helps. I'm an obliging person . . . That means helpful in this case.'

'Ar nar what it means, yer clever little gobshite. Ar's from Sunderland, not Newcastle.'

'Well, I was just going to discuss football until you mentioned them two cities,' piped up Alistair, 'but they 'aven't got a decent team between them in the same class as Leeds United.' He knew he'd stirred up a hornets nest here. Football in the north east was not just a game but a religion, and joking aside, Alistair also knew that both clubs had the most fanatical supporters in the world – along with Leeds United supporters of course.

'How can yer follow that shite?' said Don derisively. 'Especially when yer up here so often where there's the finest club in the world on your doorstep.'

'Whey, ar winna argue with that,' agreed Roy.

Sunderland football team was the only thing these two bullshitters had in common.

'Excuse me,' Frank intervened. 'Aren't we forgetting something here?'

'Like what Frank?' questioned Roy.

'Newcastle United, that's who.'

'Whey no, we're talking aboot football!'

'Yer cheeky little sod! Ar've a good mind to drop yer off that bridge.'

'Yer'll 'ave to catch me first. No – ar's actually being a bit harsh aboot your team Frank. Ar heard they got a corner last week, or was that just a rumour?'

'That's it yer bugger!' said Frank getting to his feet. 'Yer ganning ower that bridge!'

Roy ran off, but only went a short distance, he knew Frank wouldn't be in pursuit. 'Ar was only joking man!' he called as he made his way back.

'Look at the big girls blouse,' scorned Alistair whilst Roy was still out of earshot. 'He's like a big kid. He supports Sunderland until they lose a few games on the trot – which is quite often I might add – an' then he says he's thinking of supporting Newcastle – just fer the change like. That's if they've had a good run . . . He's a two faced bugger is our Roy. 'Do you like football Mrs Shand? I was thinking . . . '

'Steady on lad,' interrupted Don.

Alistair carried on, 'If you supported Middlesborough, we'd 'ave covered all the teams up here.'

'No son, ar's the same as bald eagle here,' stated Olga, looking at Don. 'Ar support Sunderland.'

Roy had rejoined the group, his mouth back in gear immediately. 'Ar wish ar'd brought me sunglasses,' he announced. 'Don . . . why divent yer wear a hat man? The sun's relecting on your cranium an' it's blinding me. You should 'ave a licence fer that heed.'

'Gan away an' shite, yer little whipper snapper! It's time you learned to respect yer elders. I fought in the war fer the likes o' ye.'

'What war was that then?' mocked Roy. 'The Boer War?'

'Is that the only joke yer nar?'

'Ar'd give in if I were you,' Olga advised Don. 'You're fighting a losing battle there.'

'Divent worry aboot me. The young bugger might 'ave a lot of lip, but they could quite easily become swollen. Ar've not forgotten my boxing skills. I wasn't middleweight champion fer nowt yer nar.'

'Yer divent frighten me Don,' boasted Roy. 'As long as yer dinna nut me with that massive bald heed of yours.'

'Ar won't need to. A quick right hook an' yer'll be asleep fer the rest of the day.'

'Before you mek the mistake in thinking ar's a push ower – I have to convey to you by law, that I am a black belt karate expert, and that it would be utter folly, especially with ye being an old fogey, to attempt an assault on my person.'

'The only black belt ye have is the one holding yer trousers up.'

'Ar'll tell yer this an' all,' added Roy. 'Me favver was a boxer.'

'He wasn't was he?' said Don looking non plussed.

'Aye, he was . . . an me mother was a cocker spaniel.'

'That's it! Ha way Olga, ar canna stand nee more. Let's gan an' get a cuppa. On second thoughts, ar'll 'ave a double whiskey – ar need it.'

'We'll walk down with yer,' announced Roy. 'Mek sure yer safe like.'

'It's a bloody tale! Come on Olga, ar need a piddle. Ar'll see yer later Frank.'

'Aye, cheerio,' acknowledged Frank, trying to keep a straight face.

'Bye Mr an' Mrs Shand!' shouted Roy after them. 'See yer later!'

'Ar hope not!' replied Don walking straight ahead, not bothering to turn round.

Well out of earshot Frank laughed, shaking his head in disbelief. 'Bah, you revel in getting Don going divent yer? Ar've noticed that afore.'

'Aye, yer not wrong Frank, but he loves it really. He's game fer a bit of bullshit is old bald eagle. They're a grand couple Don an' Olga . . . Fer macams like.'

'Are we gonna get these rosehips weighed in or not?' sighed Alistair.

'Aye, get thee pipe man, ar's just finishing my conversation with Mr Noland.'

Frank got to his feet again. 'Whey, it's time ar was away home anyway, so yer might as well get round the castle an' get some brass fer yer hips. Ar'll catch yer later.'

'See yer Frank.'

'Bye Mr Noland,' added Alistair.

Haversacks thrown over their shoulders, they set off in the opposite direction towards the Butts. Reaching the top of the Butts, they turned left past the Pack Horse and crossed the market place round to the large open gates leading into the castle grounds. Walking a short distance up the path, they veered left to the weighing room. Entering through the door, their haversacks were taken from them and weighed by a man holding a contraption with a hook. A needle pointed to the weight and the lads were paid accordingly, after they'd emptied the rosehips into the large wooden crate. Roy always managed a few more coppers than Alistair on account of him having a larger haversack.

After leaving the castle grounds, the lads crossed the main road and went into the public convenience where they found Clive Forth inside. He worked for the local council and was cleaning the dark blue ceramic tiles above the urinal.

'Hey up lads, how's it ganning?'

'Champion Clive. Me an' our Alistair 'ave been hipping. Just been ower the castle grounds getting weighed in like. A few hours an' we'll be bopping the night away in Jo Jo's. Where are you bound tonight Clive, down the boozer?'

'Ar certainly will be bonny lad, it's payday. Ar'll start off up in the west end, an' 'ave one in the Grey Bull, back down 'ere fer a pint in the Phoenix, then ower the road to the Pack Horse fer one. Then the Queens fer a quickie, an' ending up in the club fer the last hour. Ar canna wait.'

'Is your job well paid then?' asked Roy.

'Nar, not really, but overtime at the weekend boosts me pay packet.'

'When yer work Sundays, do yer get time an' a turd?'

'Bah, yer scraping the barrel with that joke Roy lad.'

'It's better than scraping the shite up.'

'Aye, yer right there, but yer've heard the saying 'aven't yer? Where there's muck, there's money.'

'Our Alistair'll nar that saying. It's a Yorkshire one if ar's not mistekken.'

'Aye it is,' confirmed Alistair. 'It's said many a time back home.'

'Anyway, ar winna be cleaning shit 'ouses an' sweeping the streets all me life,' proclaimed Clive. 'I'm studying law yer nar. Plenty of brass in that game – after yer've qualified like – an' that teks some deeing. In fact, on paper, it looks a bit ower ambitious. It's ganna tek aboot seven years swotting.'

'At least you're trying,' said Alistair encouraging him. 'Everyone should have a dream – a goal in life.'

'Divent mention goals in front of your Roy. He doesn't nar what yer talking aboot – him supporting Sunderland like.'

That was like a red rag to a bull with Roy. Not that he needed an excuse for the verbal diarrhoea to start flowing.

'Whey, what's a shit 'ouse cleaner nar aboot football? Studying law my backside . . . Yer'd be better off studying the life cycle of a dung beetle, because yer'll still be cleaning this khazie when yer sixty five.'

Clive wished that he'd kept his big mouth shut. He didn't even attempt a funny reply, knowing full well he was no match for

Roy's sharp wit. 'We'll just see if ar get anywhere. It winna be through lack o' trying if ar don't,' he said somewhat subdued.

'Ar's only kidding Clive man. With your determination, yer can do anything yer put yer mind to.'

This statement from Roy surprised both Clive and Alistair, leaving them both speechless.

Chapter 3

The boys set off up the street for home, passing the fire station and the town hall.

Alistair turning to Roy said, 'I thought Jekyll an' Hyde was in the toilets back there. One minute you're jumping down poor Clive's throat an' in the next breath you're praising him.'

'Aye, he's a canny lad is Clive, wouldn't harm a fly. Ar realised I'd given him too much stick ower his job. After all, someone's got to clean up the shit – it canna be much fun like. Ar remember him from school . . .'

Alistair knew this not to be true, Clive was at least six years older than Roy.

Roy went on, 'On sports day in the one hundred yards race . . . Clive never came first, or even second for that matter, he always came **turd**.'

'You couldn't resist could you? And there's me thinking yer'd turned over a new leaf.'

'Whey someone's got to be the Stanhope personality. We can't all be boring like ye.'

'Trouble with you though, is yer go too far an' don't know when to stop,' derided Alistair.

'Yer nar the trouble with ye, an' ar've telt yer this afore. You worry too much. Lighten up boy an' enjoy yer sen.'

'The old boys aren't there,' commented Alistair as they passed the bench.

'The three wise men'll be 'aving afters in the Grey Bull,' Roy sagely replied.

'Wasn't there three of them knocking about last year?' questioned Alistair.

'Aye, Alf Smith was a big mate of theirs. Unlucky Alf they used to call him. Lived down the lane until he kicked the bucket.'

'How did he die, was it natural causes?'

'Nar, it was tragic really. He won the pools like, but the poor bugger dropped dead the same night. The irony of it is – he was drinking a can of Long-Life at the time. Only a month earlier, he'd been complaining of pains in his back, so the old boys had rubbed lard on it for him. Aye . . . it was all downhill after that.'

Alistair let out a groan, 'I wish I'd never asked.'

'Ar's sorry Ali,' chuckled Roy. 'Joking aside though, Alf has been ill, but ar've heard he's on the mend now.'

PC Fowler came round the corner of Paragon Street, almost colliding with the boys. He was out of uniform and dressed in a smart grey suit, white shirt and tie. His hair was slicked back with Brylcreem and he smelled like a puffs parlour. 'Alright lads? Keeping out of mischief are we?'

'Course we are constable,' replied Roy. "Ave yer painted any masterpieces lately **Constable**? Ar hope yer don't mind me asking, but is that the new uniform? Because if it is, my granda's paying far too much in rates.'

'Still as funny as ever Roy. If you must know,' PC Fowler went on to explain, 'I'm going to meet my girlfriend in Crook. We're off dancing tonight at the policeman's ball.'

"Ave yer polished yer bobby's helmet?'

'Good job I'm off duty Osborne.'

"Ave yer got plenty o' money on yer constable? Yer'll need more thana few **coppers** to treat the young lady mind. Will the dance band be playing any Elvis numbers like **Jailhouse** Rock?'

'Have you quite finished with the corny jokes?'

'Aye, sorry PC Fowler, ar canna help meself at times. Ar hope you have a good night anyway.'

'Well thank you. I'll see you later and be good.'

'We'll try. Cheerio constable. He's not bad fer a copper,' said Roy turning to Alistair. 'He's got a cushy little number posted up here mind. If a turnip gans missing from a farmers field, it's a major crime round here. He gets that house up Paragon Street an' he doesn't 'ave to pay any rent fer it yer nar.'

'I've heard that in his spare time his hobby is painting,' commented Alistair. 'Particularly the local scenery. His favourite artist is **Constable**.'

'What a crap joke! Ar've already done that one. Yer not much **cop** are yer? Now ar nar why I tell the jokes our kid. Ar think yer should leave the funnys to me. Ye just stick to being a boring Yorkshire git.'

'You know your trouble Roy? There's only you thinks you're comical.'

'Arraway an' shite – yer just jealous man.'

They arrived home a few minutes after grandad, just in time for tea.

'Did yer get plenty o' rosehips picked lads?' inquired nana.

'Yes we did nana,' enthused Alistair. 'We managed to fill our haversacks to the top before we got them weighed in down the castle.'

'Whey, don't you be spending the brass on tomorrows trip hinny, yer've got that money separate. What yer've earned today an' any more money you earn, yer put away fer Stanhope Show. You an' all Roy, keep it separate.'

'Ar nar that nana, but ar wouldn't worry aboot our Alistair spending brass – he's as tight as a duck's behind – Yorkshire folk are famous fer it.'

'I'm not tight,' protested Alistair. 'I'm just careful. We're not all like you. You've got to spend yer last penny 'cause it burns a hole in yer pocket. There's never no tomorrow with you.'

'Whey, that's what brass is for bonny lad. Last year you came back from the trip with as much money as yer went with. Where's the fun in that? Too busy mekking sandcastles on the beach weren't yer?'

'Well this year's gonna be different, 'cause I'm off on the rides in the amusement park with you. I'll show yer.'

'When yer've stopped bickering ye two,' chided auntie Kitty,

'Get up to the bathroom an' wash yer hands – granda should be finished in there by now.'

The boys waited at the bottom of the stairs as grandad came down. 'Nar then lads, have yer had a fruitful day? Ar hear yer've been rose hipping.'

'Yes we have grandad,' Alistair told him eagerly. 'We got a haversack full each didn't we Roy?'

'Aye, we did alright like.'

'Yer'll be able to treat yer old grandad come Stanhope show weekend, if yer pick enough hips by then. Ar was wondering where my beer money was coming from. Yer nana an' Kitty spend all my brass,' he chuckled.

'Why don't any of the men go on the trip grandad?' asked Alistair.

He winked at Alistair, 'Because it's the only time we can get any peace an' quiet lad. Divent tell 'em ar said that like . . . The men get to stay in the club all day,' he whispered. 'We 'ave a darts competition an' a domino knockout, all sorts — An' maybe the odd pint or two . . . It's the only day of the year we divent get earache fer being home late from the club. Here,' he said handing them half a crown each. 'That's fer tomorrows trip. You 'ave a good time an' ar hope the weather stays fine fer yers.'

'Thanks grandad,' they said as they ran up the stairs, glad that they'd bumped into him on the way down.

The fish and chips tasted even better than usual on this Friday night. What, with the rosehip money and grandad's half a crown, things were looking good all round. Later on, they'd be dancing at Jo Jo's, having not had to lie anymore about where they were going, because auntie Kitty had accepted for some unknown reason, that nothing untoward went on at the snack bar.

Bert and Betty, who ran the cafe, were strict with the local lads and lasses. No smoking for under sixteens and, being a small village, lying about your age was a complete waste of time. Alcohol was certainly banned and woe betide anyone turning up smelling of drink – they'd be shown the door sharpish.

'Divent forget mind – back by half past nine tonight!' warned Kitty. 'Yer can have yer sens an early night. It'll be a long day tomorrow, yer divent want to be half asleep.'

'Ar beg to differ mother,' expressed Roy. 'If ar slept on that coach all the way to Whitley Bay, an' didn't 'ave to listen to all those excited, smelly kids, ar wouldn't complain.'

'Whey, it wasn't so long ago ye were one o' them excited kids.'

'You mean last year don't you auntie Kitty?' joked Alistair.

'Ar grew up long afore ye!' argued Roy. 'You, yer southerner – you were still in nappies when ar was already working round the farm!'

'Southerner?' cried Alistair indignantly. 'I'm from Leeds, not London – Geordie boy.'

'Ar've telt yer afore Alistair,' reproached his auntie Kitty. 'We're Weardalers, not Geordies.'

'I'm sorry auntie Kitty, it's your Roy – he gets me going.'

'Whey, ar thought yer'd be used to him by now. He could make a vicar swear mind, that yan.'

'Excuse me, but ar think yer'll find I'm right,' corrected Roy. 'Leeds is definately south of Stanhope.'

'Clear the table ye two,' ordered nana. 'An' give the bickering a rest, life's too short.'

After doing as they were told, the boys went upstairs to their bedroom.

Grandad had settled down to read the Northern Echo. Later, he would put on his black shiny boots in readiness for taking Lassie for a walk down the dean bottom. Grandad was always meticulous when it came to his footwear. Not a day would go by without a disciplined spit and polish of his boots and shoes. You could see your face in them. This attention to detail had been passed down to his son Johnny, Alistair's father. He in turn passed it on to Alistair. 'You can always tell a man by his shoes.'

Roy got out his birds egg collection from under the bed and showed them to Alistair. There was an assortment of different colours and sizes. Alistair's favourites were the speckled ones.

Roy had shown him how to 'blow' the eggs. Blowing meant getting rid of the contents. This entailed pricking the egg at both ends. Then, giving it a good blow at one end to get rid of the liquid contents through the hole at the other end.

The collecting of some birds eggs was illegal, but Roy and Alistair didn't look too deeply into which ones they were.

'Right, ar's off fer a wash,' declared Roy, sliding his box of eggs back under the bed. 'An' divent think of pinching any when ar's gone. I nar exactly how many's in the box.'

'Well it never entered me head to take any, but I just might do now you've **egged** me on.'

'Alistair!' cried Roy in amazement. 'Yer've **cracked** a joke! It's not like ye – yer must be coming out of yer **shell**. 'Ave yer got any more **poultry yolks** like that?'

'Just hurry up if you're going in that bathroom will yer? I want to use it.'

'Alright, keep yer 'air on **chuck**. Divent sweat, ar's ganning.'

Alistair picked up the Beano from the window sill and sat on the bed. He could hear Roy singing in the bathroom. Even though Roy was tone deaf, it didn't deter him from bellowing out Three Steps to Heaven. Roy liked to think of himself as Stanhope's own Eddie Cochrane, Roy's favourite singer.

Alistair thought it sounded like a cat going through a mangle, not that he'd ever witnessed such a thing, or even wanted to.

Finished washing, Roy took grandads aftershave from the bathroom cabinet. Hoping that no one downstairs would smell it on him – he dabbed a little under his chin. He thought to himself how he'd now have to leave by the front door and hope and pray that he wouldn't be called back for any reason.

'Right boy, it's all yours,' said Roy emerging from the bathroom.

'I hope you haven't left your usual tidemark round the sink.'

'Nar, ar've wiped round it with a flannel – not that it needed it like. By the way, yer powder puff is in the airing cupboard.'

'I think you'll find that that's yours. After all, they call yer the Stanhope puff.'

'Ooh, touchy boy. An' divent be using me granda's aftershave either, he'll gan spare.'

'You mean you've been at it an' he'll notice if any more goes missing. Well, don't be worrying on that score, I'll not be pinching his aftershave, I smell nice enough. The lasses at Jo Jo's seem to think so. It fair knackers me out all that dancing. As soon as I sit down, there's another young lady pulling me up onto the dance floor again.'

'Stop trying to talk like me bonny lad, it doesn't become yer. Ar've got that certain charisma that nee one'll ever match. Ar's a bird magnet man, so you just leave the chicks to me. Besides, yer've only had aboot half a dozen dances down at Jo Jo's all summer. Yer still a bairn man, way out of yer league.'

'If you say so, God's gift,' sighed Alistair. 'I'm off for me wash. I'll leave you in peace to put yer mascara an' lipstick on. Are yer knickers dry? Don't you be putting damp ones on, yer'll catch yer death o' cold.'

'Arraway an' shite man.'

Alistair was soon finished in the bathroom. Not for him, standing and preening himself in front of the mirror for all eternity – unlike someone not a million miles away from him.

'We're off!' shouted Roy as they opened the front door.

'Whey, mek sure you're back on time an' behave yer sens!' shouted auntie Kitty.

'Will do mother, divent worry!' replied Roy, closing the door behind him in haste.

'Save one of them lasses fer Roy, Alistair!' came a voice from across the road. 'Ar nar he's not very popular like. It must be that ugly mug of his!'

The voice belonged to Lottie Parsons who was sitting on her window sill. She loved teasing the lads, especially Roy, because he in turn would give Lottie plenty of stick back.

'Did you hear an old woman's voice then our kid?' said Roy, looking round, anywhere but at Lottie.

'Hoy! Less of the old, yer cheeky bugger. How's my favourite boyfriend today Alistair?'

Alistair blushed. 'I'm fine thank you Mrs Parsons.'

'Bah, yer like yer women mature, divent yer our Ali? That old dodo bird ower there,' sneered Roy.

'Arraway with yer, yer cheeky bugger,' protested Lottie.

'Admit it Lottie . . . Yer no spring chicken are yer? The only thing ye have in common with a chicken is yer name, and yer do look like a parsons nose.'

Lottie moved swiftly off the window sill, shaking a fist at Roy. 'Ar'll swing fer ye, bugger lugs!' she shouted after him, suppressing a smile as the boys ran off down the Square laughing.

'Evening Mrs Lister.'

'Aye.'

'Did yer see 'er slippers Ali? She always wears them wi' the zip up an' the fur round the top. Ar bet she's had them on fer the last ten years. Ar've never seen her in any others.'

'Stop exaggerating Roy.'

'Ar's not man. Yer've seen me mothers slippers 'aven't yer? They're exactly the same ones, the only difference is me mothers 'ave got white fur round the top, while Mrs Lister's fur 'as gone yellow. Too tight to buy another pair man. It's not as if she's short of a bob or two either.'

'Give it a rest will you? You're like an old washer woman. Have you ever thought that Mrs Lister's slippers could 'ave yellow jaundice?'

'Whey, yer silly bugger, yer getting as daft as me now,' chuckled Roy. 'Ha way, let's gan round the playing field, ar's not had a fag all day.'

The sun was still warm on the boy's faces. This time of year, the sun was sinking a little more each day, making the night-time darkness descend that bit earlier each evening, giving clues of autumn approaching just around the corner.

'Bah, it's busy round here tonight our Roy,' remarked Alistair. 'I thought this time of an evening was always quiet.'

'Whey, folks are mekking the most of it bonny lad. A lot of 'em bring a picnic tea. The kids love it, being able to stay longer because it's the school holidays. You give it ten or fifteen minutes an' they'll start wandering off home. After all, they've got to get ready fer tomorrows trip. The kids'll be like you tonight . . . unable to sleep fer the excitement. There'll be a few smelly bedrooms tonight, that's fer sure.'

'You were the same when you were younger,' stated Alistair. 'I suppose it's a bit like Christmas Eve really,' he reflected. 'You lay awake half the night, willing the morning to arrive so's yer can rip the paper off yer presents. It doesn't matter that someone's spent ages carefully folding over the sheets an' neatly creasing the corners an' sellotaping 'em down . . .'

'Just divent ye be farting all night, stinking my bedroom out,' warned Roy. 'You shouldn't still be excited ower a silly day trip at your age.'

'I'm not, an' I don't lose sleep anymore,' Alistair lied. 'But I am looking forward to the outing all the same.'

''Ave yer seen old Mrs Ratcliffe ower there?' said Roy, nodding in the direction of the river. 'She's sat 'aving a picnic with her two granddaughters. Look, she's got nee teeth in. Look at 'er tackling that tomato our kid. She looks like a bulldog chewing a wasp. Why she doesn't put 'er teeth in, ar divent nar.'

'Well me nana sometimes leaves her teeth out.'

'Aye, but that's at home, not when she's out. She'll 'ave 'em in tomorrow alright. She'll need 'em to chew them mussels an' whelks an' all that seafood shite.'

Alistair had just sat down in the playing field shelter when a young lad asked him to retrieve his ball from the paddling pool. As on many occasions before, Alistair threw stones behind the floating ball, thus causing ripples which pushed the ball to the edge of the pool. He and Roy would never take their shoes and socks off and venture in, because the slippery bottom of the neglected pool was lethal.

The boy thanked Alistair gleefully and ran off. Alistair returned to the shelter.

Roy was in the toilet at the end of the shelter puffing away on a cigarette as if his life depended on it. Alistair had tried smoking, but didn't enjoy the experience. He was visualising Roy now . . . He'd be admiring his 'good looks' in the mirror there, attempting to blow smoke rings into the air, oblivious to the fact that no one else thought him good looking.

Roy emerged from the toilet and swaggered towards Alistair, legs apart like John Wayne, cocksure of himself as usual. 'Whey, ar walked into the bog an' ar was surprised to see somebody 'ad stuck a picture of Tony Curtis up on the wall . . . Then ar realised it was my reflection in the mirror.'

'Frankenstein's monster's reflection you mean. With that stupid crew cut o' yours – all you need is a bolt through yer neck.'

'At least ar's not a stick insect. What d'you weigh anyway? Aboot five stone, wet through ar'll bet. An' that long greasy hair o' yours . . . it's like ganning aboot with a mobile mop. Me granda could use you as a pipe cleaner.'

Roy had hit a sore point with Alistair. 'I can't help being skinny. I eat plenty.'

'Tha' wants to get some drippin' an' bread down yer man – puts hairs on yer chest like mine. Birds gan crazy running their fingers through it, they love a manly chest.'

'Yer lying bugger! You've got no hairs on yer chest at all, an' you won't 'ave either for a good few years yet.'

'Whey, ar've got one or two. Yer canna see 'em 'cause they're fair. Ar might stick some black boot polish on 'em . . . '

'That's a good idea, then all them birds yer go out with can brush up against 'em. After all, anyone daft enough to go out with you must be a scrubber.'

'Envy'll eat yer away Yorky boy.'

'I'm not envious,' said a smug Alistair. 'I've got my admirers.'

'Dream on son . . . Ar tell yer what though, some of my dynamic self confidence is definately rubbing off on yer. Ar's grooming yer well fer when yer grows up like.'

'Get lost! If I'm owt like you in a few years time I'll shoot me sen.'

'Ah . . . we'll see bonny lad, we'll see. Ha way, let's gan down the street.'

They walked by the waterside, heading for the market place, occasionally looking in the river when hearing the splash of a trout as it surfaced to snatch an unlucky insect.

The market place was quiet when the lads arrived at six thirty. They sat themselves down on the steps of the old stone cross. Roy, much to his annoyance, was being attacked by midges. There seemed to be an abundance of the pesky things tonight. It was pleasantly warm, but not particularly humid – you'd certainly never have expected a plague of the damn things.

'I've noticed you're attracting an army of midges our Roy,' remarked Alistair. 'Mind you, it's well known they like to hover round shit.'

'Hey lad, watch yer sen. You're asking fer a bunch o' fives,' said an increasingly irritated Roy, brushing the midges away from his face.

'Oh aye, you an' whose army?'

'Ar divent need an army. They divent call me the Stanhope fighting machine fer nowt yer nar.'

Dennis Melly was passing. He was a good friend of the lads grandad and was a committee man at Stanhope Working Mens Club. 'How's it ganning lads?' he said as he sat down next to them on the steps.

'Champion,' acknowledged Roy. 'We're just aboot to paint the town red.'

'By that yer mean yer going to Jo Jo's, right?'

'Aye, yer've hit the nail on the head Mr Melly. We're hitting the local groovy night club. It's compulsory fer me to make an appearance mind . . . Bert an' Betty pay me to gan yer nar . . . They say that the local personality attracts the birds an' boosts their trade like.'

'Take no notice of him Mr Melly,' said Alistair derisively.

'Divent worry son, ar nar what he's like.'

'Night club . . . ' scoffed Alistair. 'They kick us out at nine o'clock. An' as for our Roy being the main attraction – Bert's on the verge of banning him.'

'That's rubbish! Their business would gan bust ower night if they got shut o' me.'

'It's great at Jo Jo's Mr Melly, because when our Roy's rabbiting on too much – which is nearly all the time – Bert turns up the volume on the jukebox an' drowns 'im out.'

'It's all lies Mr Melly. Ar's not known as the Stanhope orator fer nowt yer nar. When ar start telling my compelling stories, everyone grabs a chair an' congregates round my table.'

'Yer mean they suddenly get up an' dance or go fer a piss,' derided Alistair.

'Yer divent drink booze in there ar hope?' inquired Mr Melly, tongue in cheek. 'Or smoke that whacky baccy . . . Marry Joanna?'

'Ar think you mean marijuana,' corrected Roy.

'Whey, an' ye'd nar that wouldn't ye?'

'Only because ar've read aboot it like. The strongest thing Bert an' Betty allows in Jo Jo's is wine gums. Mind you, after three o' them our Alistair's staggering all ower the place. Last week, he ate four of 'em an' ar had to carry him home. It was getting a bit dark an' ar was stopped by PC Fowler. He must 'ave thought ar'd been robbing a grave or summat because he asked me why ar was carrying a skeleton ower me shoulder.'

'That's hilarious hedgehog head, I don't think,' groaned Alistair.

'Are ye two like this all the time?' asked Dennis.

'Aye,' replied Roy. 'It helps to pass the time. Will you be seeing me granda down the club tonight?'

'Aye, yer granda's on the door tonight. We'll be 'aving a good chat ower a few pints, chewing the cud, so to speak.'

'What's that mean Mr Melly?' asked Roy.

'Whey, sort of reflecting on things in general like.'

'An' how many pints d'yer both sup – Just out of curiosity yer nar. Four or five?'

'Maybe.'

'Aha, that means more, ar can tell. Go on . . . seven or eight?'

'Could be.'

'Blooming heck! Yer down plenty divent yer? I must say though, ar've never seen me granda come home from the club drunk. Mind you, he does say that the steward watters the beer down. Do you think he does?'

'Whey, ar couldn't say fer sure, but if he does, he wouldn't be the first. It's quite a common practice, if rumour's to be believed. I enjoy the beer, wattered down or not.'

'These committee meetings on a Sunday morning, are they just an excuse for an early pint or two?'

'Whey, no man! Serious business is discussed. The club canna run its sen yer nar.'

'These debates you have . . . What d'yer find to talk aboot like? Whose turn it is to sharpen the darts, or paint the white spots on the dominoes? Me granda says the club is too tight to buy another set or two. Is it true that the darts are so old, they've got dodo feathers fer flights? He also telt me that the last time the club was decorated, he missed it because he was in France fighting in the battle of the Somme. Mind you – ar've heard that yer let anybody in . . . '

'Only folks that are members or affiliated.'

'Whey, what aboot that scruff Albert Crane? Lives down the street, won't work an' smells like a midden, according to me granda.'

'He's a club member an' pays his subs,' stated Dennis. 'Spends a bit o' brass on beer an' all. He sits in a corner on his own. If yer divent get down wind of him, he's nee problem.'

'Well, ar divent nar where he gets all his money from . . . ' Roy was on form now. 'He's a lazy bugger – fifty eight years old an' his last job was school prefect. Ar've heard his first insurance stamp is worth more than the penny black. Apparently, he's been signing on that long, he gans on the staff Christmas party at the dole office. An' that wife of his . . . 'ave yer seen her? Bertha she's called, looks like the back end of a bus, a big fat woman. When she gans fer a night out at the club, a Pickfords removal van brings her. It's true Alistair – ask Dennis. Me granda telt me that he's got to open the double doors to squeeze her in, and that's after rubbing lard on the door frame. She sups beer out of a bucket an' all. A couple of weeks back she was in the concert room an' there was a comedian on. Whey, apparently, she laughed that much, she farted an' followed through.'

'Urgh!' grimaced Alistair. 'Did she clean it up?'

'Nar, she just carried on as if nothing had happened an' let the shite dry on her. Sent the old man to the bar when her bucket needed refilling.'

'Aye, we lost some custom that night,' said Dennis, supporting

Roy's story. 'Nee bugger dared to complain because she'd flatten 'em if they did,' he sighed. 'The Queens took some brass that night. We lost most of the concert room customers.'

'Well, who cleaned up after her then?' asked Alistair.

'Nee bugger. It was left until the following morning. Your mate Billy cleared up the mess.'

'Billy?' cried Roy incredulously.

'Whey aye, yer nar his mother cleans at the club divent yer?'

'Yes.'

'Their Billy helps her on a weekend, an' he ended up deeing all the dirty work.'

Roy's face was a picture of mischief. 'Wait till ar see him . . . He kept that quiet.'

'Whey, yer canna blame him can yer?'

'No, that's true Dennis. Ar's glad ar bumped into you Mr Melly, yer've made my day.'

'Ar've said nowt mind.'

'Understood, mum's the word.'

Dennis set off home and the boys made their way to the back of Jo Jo's cafe. It was five to seven, and they were a little early. Roy crouched beneath the window, his head bobbing up and down, trying to spy on Bert and Betty. They were sitting at a table chatting – then Bert got up and disappeared into the front room.

Roy turned and whispered to Alistair. 'Bert's gone. When he comes back, ar'll bang on the window an' mek 'em jump.'

'Aye, go on then,' said Alistair. No sooner had the words left his mouth, when he saw Bert coming up the alley towards them, a rolled up newspaper in his hand. Bert put a finger to his lips, indicating to Alistair to keep quiet. Tiptoeing towards Roy who was still crouching beneath the window, he whacked him twice on the head with the rolled up newspaper.

'Ow! What yer deeing man?'

'Oh, I'm sorry,' said Bert laughing. 'Ar didn't realise it was you Roy. I thought there was a porcupine on my window sill. Eeh . . . I enjoyed that.'

Meanwhile Betty had unlocked the door and was wondering

what all the commotion was.

'It's alright pet, ar just caught a porcupine trying to break into the cafe,' chuckled Bert.

'He's smacked me around the head with a rolled up newspaper Betty!' wailed Roy, looking for sympathy.

'Whey, you're too heavy handed our Bert,' rebuked Betty. 'You could have caused him some brain damage. No . . . cancel that last statement, it's already too late fer that.'

'Go on Betty,' whined Roy. 'Enjoy my discomfort. Stick the boot in when a man's down.'

'Orh . . . Come here hinny, let auntie Betty kiss yer heed better.'

'It's a tale,' said Roy backing off. 'Ar's fine now. It's a miracle, not even a twinge. That threat of a kiss off you really did the trick.'

'Yer cheeky bugger! Bert never complains, do yer pet?'

'Look at him,' said Roy. 'He's gone all red. I bet you kiss Betty late at night when she's tekken her teeth out, don't you Bert?'

'Ar divent need to tek me teeth out clever dick, because they're not false! Another remark like that an' yer'll be banned from the cafe.'

'A bit touchy tonight aren't we? Got out of bed the wrong side this morning did we?'

Roy knew Betty wasn't serious about banning him. She was a good sport was Betty and enjoyed a laugh – so long as you didn't go too far.

'Ha way inside everybody. We're not earning any brass stood out here kalling.'

Chapter 4

A few more lads and lasses arrived, shortly followed by Billy. Bobby Vee's, The Night Has a Thousand Eyes blared from the jukebox as Billy made his way towards Alistair and Roy's table.

'Phew! What's that smell our kid?' exclaimed Roy, pretending he hadn't seen Billy come in. 'Oh, hello Billy, how's it ganning, alright?'

'Aye, not so bad like,' he replied, delving into his pockets for some change. 'Ar'll just nip in the front, an' get me sen a Vimto. I won't be a minute.'

Alistair was idly unravelling the wax straw he'd removed from his bottle of Coca-Cola, preferring to drink the pop straight from the bottle like the older boys.

Roy got up to follow Billy and joined him at the front counter. 'Hurry up bonny lad, ar've a right thirst on. There it is again . . . ' said Roy, sniffing the air. 'It smells like shite. Can you smell owt Billy? Check yer shoes fer dog muck.'

'Ar canna smell owt, an' there's nee dog shite on my shoes,' Billy insisted, lifting each foot in turn and examining it. 'It'll be your aftershave man – it stinks to high heaven.'

Roy's attempt at getting Billy going had backfired on him. 'Divent talk wet man, it's me granda's finest aftershave. It turns all the lasses heads when ar waft past 'em.'

'Ar divent wonder their heeds turn man, they probably think a puff's just gone past when they get a sniff o' that crap.'

'Wait until ar tell me granda what you're saying aboot his aftershave. Hang on though, ar can't – He doesn't know ar've used it. Forget that last remark.'

Billy took his bottle of Vimto from the counter and returned to the jukebox room, sitting himself next to Alistair.

Meanwhile, Roy was telling Bert and Betty the tale about Billy working with his mother, cleaning the club at the weekend. How he'd kept it from them, the incident of the aftermath of Big Bertha's wet fart.

'Ar've got a joke for yer Bert,' said Roy. 'Are yer listening? Right . . . Did you hear the one aboot the Irishman who bought a two piece jigsaw puzzle? He sent it back because it didn't 'ave a picture on the box.'

'Dear me,' groaned Bert. 'Can't yer dee better than that?'

'Whey, ar thought it was funny,' grumbled Roy. 'Give us me Coca-Cola will yer? Ar's off back in the music room where ar's appreciated.'

'You do that boy, leave me an' Betty in peace to enjoy a well earned cuppa.'

'He's a miserable sod, that Bert,' complained Roy as he sat back down with the boys. 'Ar just telt him a perfectly good joke, an' he didn't even bat an eyelid. Even if he hadn't found it funny, he could've pretended an' given me a false chuckle – the money ar spend in 'ere . . . '

'Yer divent even nar a good joke man,' sneered Billy. 'How can you expect Bert to laugh at the rubbish ye come out with?'

'Ah, yer miserable shit cleaner . . . ' muttered Roy.

'What was that?'

'Nowt.'

It was quiet for a Friday night, but it was still early so the lads weren't unduly worried yet as to whether any of the local lasses would turn up.

Roy disappeared to the toilet as Bert and Betty came through from the shop front, going straight over to the jukebox. Tell Laura I Love her played as they danced cheek to cheek.

Roy returned to the table and sat back down. "Ave yer seen them? Fred Astaire an' Ginger Rogers? Watch yer divent slip a disc you old buggers!'

'What was that?' Bert shouted. 'Ar canna hear yer man!'
'Forget it,' said Roy.

The back door opened. Three local girls and two boys came in, sitting themselves at the opposite side of the room, nodding their acknowledgement of everyone in passing.

'Things are looking up chaps,' said Billy, rubbing his hands together.

Bert stopped dancing to go and serve the newcomers. Betty sat down at the lads table. 'You're quiet tonight boys,' she commented. 'Why aren't you up dancing an' enjoying yer sens?'

'We'll be up soon,' Roy assured her. 'Especially now there's a few birds to gan at.'

'Yer'll be off on the day trip tomorrow won't yer?' she asked.

'Aye,' confirmed Roy. 'Our Alistair's got his bucket an' spade packed, 'aven't yer pet?'

'Yes, it's in the bag along with your rattle an' dummy – old flower,' sneered Alistair.

'Now, now girls, no arguing in my cafe,' admonished Betty. 'Get yer sens up on that dance floor – it's compulsory. Yer not here to sit in a corner looking hag ridden.'

'Whey, ar canny dance Betty man,' protested Roy.

'Why not like?'

'Because ar've been fer a crap in your so called excuse fer a toilet, an' that Izal toilet paper's left me arse cheeks sore — It's like a blood orange. Yer should buy that soft stuff, or is that too dear?'

'Whey, you ungrateful bugger. You're lucky to have any at all. If it was up to our Bert, yer'd be wiping yer bum on old newspapers.'

'Ar can believe that an' all, the tight sod.'

'That's my husband you're talking aboot.'

'Never mind Betty . . . we all mek mistakes. Ar mean – just look at him . . . He's had the same clothes on fer the last month. Arthur Haynes is immaculately dressed aside o' Bert. He needs fumigating – sharpish like. If the health inspectors come in here an' see the state of him, they'll shut yer down.'

'Eeh, it's a good job he's in the front,' said Betty as she stood up looking extremely angry. 'Ar think ar'll nip round an' tell him what yer've been saying about him.' She winked at Billy and Alistair.

'Divent tell Bert!' pleaded Roy. 'Ar was only joking man!'

'Oh I don't nar . . . Shall I or shan't I? If you get a lass up to dance right now, ar might say nowt.'

'Nee problem,' said Roy, scrambling to his feet. He was over the other side of the room in a flash. After several seconds he led Kathy, a local shop assistant, onto the dance floor.

Johnny Tillotson's Poetry in Motion was playing as Betty pulled Alistair out of his chair, 'Come on bonny lad – you too Billy.'

When Bert came back into the room, he was surprised to see so many up and dancing. He hastened to the jukebox and selected several more records, hoping to keep everyone on their feet – hence keeping the happy upbeat atmosphere, and also being able to join in himself.

After shaking and jiving to five records, the less energetic of them were relieved when a slow, smoochy number came on. This gave them the excuse to sit back down.

Brenda Lee sang, All Alone Am I. Several couples paired up. Bert and Betty, Roy and Kathy, and Billy and Susan. Alistair was sitting on his own, trying not to show how despondent he felt. He wasn't alone for long though, because to his great surprise, a young lady approached him and asked him to dance. He certainly didn't need asking twice.

They smooched on the dance floor. Alistair wearing a blissful, smug expression on his face . . . Knowing he'd deprived Roy of taking the mickey out of him for having no one to dance with. Yes . . . it was a good feeling . . . Dancing cheek to cheek with this bird wasn't half bad either. What, with the day trip to look forward to tomorrow, everything in the garden was rosy.

A couple more slow, melodious tunes from the jukebox, and the music stopped. Everybody untangled themselves from one another and went their separate ways, either to sit down or to go and buy some liquid refreshment from the counter.

Roy was in the queue, impatient as ever. 'What's a man got to do to get a drink in this poor excuse fer a cafe? Ar's dehydrating waiting here!'

'Whey, ar divent nar what a man's got to do,' said Bert. 'But a boy will have to wait his turn like everyone else.'

That shut Roy up – only temporarily mind – but these rare fleeting moments of silence had to be savoured, as they were short lived.

'Right, what can ar get you Mr Osborne?' asked Bert when Roy reached the front of the queue.

'Whey ar'll 'ave a clothes brush fer starters. I've been waiting that long, ar's covered in cobwebs.'

'Less of the cheek. Do yer want serving or not? There's people waiting.'

'Aye, three Coca-Colas please.'

'Oh, I'm sorry, we've just sold the last bottle. We had a bit of a rush on yer nar.'

'Whey, yer should pay more attention to yer stock tekking then! Yer not very efficient at running a business are yer?'

'Please accept my humblest apologies Mr Osborne. Human error appears to have entered into the equation in this instance.'

'What are you rambling on aboot? Give me three Vimtos instead.'

'Now then . . . Vimto . . . ' muttered Bert, scratching his head, searching beneath the counter. 'I'm sure there's some here somewhere . . . Betty!'

'Yes my dear,' she said, emerging from the store room.

'Where's the Vimtos?'

'Have yer looked under the counter?'

'Aye, there's none there.'

'We've sold out then.'

'Dear me, this is rather embarrassing Mr Osborne. We seem to have taken our eye off the ball, I'm very sorry.'

'Ar divent nar what sort of shop you're running,' derided Roy, 'But ar nar one thing – It's shite!'

'Now, now, there's no need for that language sir. I've already said I'm sorry.'

'What yer got to drink then that's not sold out?'

'Well, let me see . . . We have milk, water, and this container of fresh chilled orange juice you see before you.'

'Three glasses of that watered down orange juice then. Hurry up an' all, ar's parched.'

Bert put a glass beneath the orange juice tap, but nothing came out. 'That's odd, it's not pouring through.'

'Ar dinna believe this!' exclaimed Roy. 'If another cafe opened up, you'd be out of business by the next day. That's your trouble – yer've nee competition. Ar think ar'll open one up in a couple o' years. Ar'll show yer how it's done.'

'You've no idea lad. You wouldn't last two minutes in this game. The hard work involved in running a cafe would be too much fer the likes o' ye . . . Betty! This orange won't flow through!'

'That's 'cause the tap's broken. A man's coming out to look at it. I'm sorry, ar should've telt yer.'

Roy shook his head in disbelief. 'Am I on Candid Camera or summat? What is there left to drink now? Are yer down to that cactus in the front window?'

'There's no need to carry on Mr Osborne, we still have milk or tap watter.'

'Ar'll try again . . . Three glasses of milk please, if yer can manage that.'

'What the hell's that?' cried Roy incredulously as the milk glugged out in lumps. 'It's a glass of bloody cheese! It's all curdled man!'

'Oh dear . . . Betty must've left it out of the fridge in the sun. I'm sorry aboot this.'

'I'm ganna wake up in a minute . . . ar must be dreaming, or having a nightmare more like. Ar just don't believe it. Three glasses of watter it is then, unless yer've had that turned off as well. Gone to the dogs this place . . . ' he muttered as he carried away three glasses of water.

'Hoy, Roy! Yer forgot these!' shouted Bert as he placed three bottles of Coca-Cola on the counter.

'Whey, you bas . . . . !'

'Ah ah, watch yer language bonny lad,' Bert warned him.

'An' they say I'm like a big kid,' sighed Roy.

By this time Betty had rejoined Bert and they chuckled together, well pleased with their little jape.

'Pair of bloody two year olds,' grumbled Roy, his sense of humour having passed him by on this occasion.

'We thought you'd gone home,' said Billy. 'What took yer so long? Did yer nip outside fer a quickie wi' one of yer many admirers?'

'Don't ask, it's a long story . . . Bert an' Betty tekking the piss. Whose turn is it fer the jukebox?' said Roy, hastily changing the subject.

'Whey, ar put the last three records on,' stated Billy.

Roy turned to Alistair, 'It must be your turn kidder. Come on Ali, get in yer pocket an' prove to us it's not all true aboot all you Yorkshiremen being tight as ducks arses – Or are yer pockets sewn up?'

'Hark at the pot calling the kettle black,' mocked Alistair. 'You're not known as the Stanhope miser fer nowt yer nar.'

'Arraway with yers. Ar's generous to a fault, it's well known in these parts.'

'Whey, it's the first ar've heard is that,' derided Billy. 'Yer wouldn't part with yer own shite if yer didn't have to.'

'Bollocks! What complete crap!'

Roy and Billy hadn't noticed Alistair leaving the table during their short altercation. Looking up from the table now, they were surprised to see him smooching on the dance floor with Gillian, a local girl who lived only yards away from Jo Jo's on Front Street. At fifteen, she was three years older than Alistair, and still went to school in Wolsingham, a village six miles away. A school bus transported the youngsters there every weekday, due to Stanhope not having a secondary school. Roy and Billy were pupils there.

'Whey, he's getting bold is Yorky boy. It's only a month since he was sitting in a corner, a bag o' nerves, shaking like a shite-ing dog. Getting too big fer his boots, that bugger.'

'Do ar detect a hint o' jealousy creeping in Roy boy?' scorned Billy.

'Gan away with yer. The stud is resting temporarily. Ar'll show the Yorkshire git how it's done . . . ' said Roy getting up and crossing the room, winding his way through the couples on the dance floor.

Billy watched him talking to Kathy Arnold. It was several minutes before Roy returned looking some what dejected.

'What's up Roy?' asked Billy. 'Did the Stanhope stud get knocked back then?'

'Who, me? Never!'

'Whey, how come she's not up dancing with yer then? Try explaining that one – Stanhope stud.'

'Ar didn't gan an' ask her fer a dance.'

'Yer lying bugger! Yer saw your Alistair dancing with a bird an' yer were green wi' envy. That's why yer shot ower the room to chat up Kathy, but she gave yer the elbow.'

'Ar did nothing of the sort, clever clogs. If yer must nar, ar went ower to ask her the price of something in the shop that she works in.'

'Bah, that's pathetic! Ar've heard it all now boyo.'

Alistair rejoined the lads at the table. He sat down looking well pleased with himself.

'Bah, yer were quick off the mark there Ali lad,' said Billy, slapping Alistair on the back.

'Well, you've either got it or you haven't Billy . . . What can I say?'

'Listen to him,' scorned Roy, venomously, not being in the best of moods. 'He dances with an ugly schoolgirl an' thinks he's Casanova.'

'No I don't yer grumpy sod!' retorted Alistair. How come you weren't up on the dance floor wifh a bird anyway?'

'Because ar's saving me sen fer the Whitley Bay lasses – an' besides, there's nee chicks worth bothering with here.'

Billy coughed in an exaggerated manner, choking on his Coca-Cola in the process. 'Whey, divent believe a word of it Alistair! He went ower to ask Kathy fer a dance an' she knocked him back. Sent him packing with his tail between his legs, chin scraping the floor.'

'Rubbish! Ar've telt yer man, ar didn't ask her fer a dance – it was on other business.'

'Oh aye, an' I'm a china man.'

'No more money in the jukebox ladies and gentlemen – it's ten to nine!' announced Betty.

She and Bert locked up the cafe at nine o'clock sharp. Staying open late meant very long days for the pair of them, so any folks loitering behind were not tolerated. The local lads and lasses didn't even try to hang about, knowing it was a waste of time. Besides, they were all truly greatful to Bert and Betty for opening late just for them, so taking liberties was not on the agenda.

Ater the usual cheerios, the boys set off up the street for home. Billy turned right into Paragon Street and went on up to Ashcroft, having already arranged to meet Roy and Alistair in the market place the next morning in readiness for the coaches departure at eight o'clock. Not that they would leave on time anyway. Every year, without exception, someone was late.

Roy was noticeably quiet on the way home – it hadn't been one of his best nights. The Stanhope stud had had a limp night, and his ego was a little deflated.

Alistair couldn't help feeling rather smug, having faired much better. He loved going to Jo Jo's now. Having shook off his initial nervous reservations, his confidence had soared, much to Roy's displeasure.

'Hello lads, had a good night?' greeted nana as they stepped through the front door.

'A smashing night nana,' replied Alistair, still grinning from ear to ear.

'It was too quiet fer my liking,' grumbled Roy. 'It's ganning downhill fast, is that place. There's too many outsiders getting in.'

It was obvious to Alistair that Roy was having a dig at him out of jealousy, but he chose not to say anything.

'What shoes will yer be wearing fer tomorrows outing?' auntie Kitty asked the boys.

'I'll go in my black pair,' Alisatir replied. 'Nana polished them for me yesterday.'

'I'll be ganning in me winkle pickers,' stated Roy. 'Ar'll nip upstairs an' get 'em an' give 'em a quick polish.'

'Do you have to wear them stupid things?' admonished his mother. 'Yer'll end up tripping ower them an' doing yer sen an injury.'

'Whey, ar like 'em. They're all the fashion fer us groovy men. We canna all be square like our Alistair.'

'At least with the shoes our Alistair wears, he'll not end up with deformed feet like ye – yer daft 'apporth.'

'Winkle pickers **used** to be all the rage in Leeds years ago,' mocked Alistair. 'But they're out of fashion now. Roy's stuck in the past. It doesn't matter anyway . . . everyone's out of date up here,' he sneered.

Roy was fuming. 'Whey, nearly all the lads wear winkle pickers! They're not out of date here boy, so if yer divent like the way we dress – bog off back to Yorkshire!'

'Stop bickering ye two,' chided nana. 'Come an' get yer suppers, yer've a long day ahead of you tomorrow. It wouldn't do yer no harm yo have an early night either. Leave yer nose pickers – or whatever yer call 'em – on the hearth, an' ar'll polish 'em – or yer granda will – first thing in the morning.'

The lads were in bed by a quarter to eleven, sitting up reading comics.

It wasn't long before Roy broke the silence with his usual cockiness. 'Ar'll show yer how to pull the birds tomorrow bonny lad. Whitley Bay won't nar what's hit them.'

'Pull birds? What's that supposed to mean? Are yer taking a collar an' lead an' going walkies down the sea front with 'em? Mind you, that's all you can pull . . . dogs.'

'Ah . . . we'll see boy. Ar got mobbed last year.'

'I thought you said it was pouring with rain an' that everyone stayed home last trip.'

'Oh yes, that's right . . . ar meant the year afore like.'

'Ha ha, yer trip up on yer own lies hedgehog head.'

'No ar divent – Ar just got the years mixed up man.'

'I'll believe you, where thousands wouldn't. Is your mate from school going, Stuart Regent?'

'Aye, he's a canny lad is Stuart. He tried to wriggle out of it like me, but it was no good. Still, we could 'ave a laugh. He's not bad at chatting the birds up either. Not up to my level, but he does alright like. He wears winkle pickers an' all an' he greases his hair back. He's a bit of a rocker is Stuart.'

'It'll be like a **teddy** bears picnic,' joked Alistair.

'Whey, there'll only be ye that's looking square. Yer've nee chance with the chicks sonny boy.'

'Well how the heck are you gonna attract the lasses with yer winkle pickers on an' grandad's old demob suit, not to mention yer porcupine haircut.'

'Just wait an' see, Yorky. Ye stick to building yer sandcastles an' paddling in the sea.'

'I've told you, I'm going to the Spanish City with you an' the other lads.'

'Fine, so long as yer nar yer'll be out of yer depth. Ar's off to sleep now,' said Roy pulling the covers up under his chin. Ar's tired an' need to be fresh fer my female admirers tomorrow. Ye won't sleep, yer'll be ower excited.

'I will,' stated Alistair indignantly. 'A day trip'll not keep me awake,' he lied while having that same feeling of excitement he experienced on Christmas Eve. He tossed and turned for a full two hours, before sleep finally overcame him.

'It's seven o'clock,' announced auntie Kitty standing at the bedroom door.

'Ar'll be two minutes,' murmured Roy, turning over.

Alistair shot out of bed straight away and was first in the bathroom, excited at the prospect of the day ahead. He sang to himself as he washed. The sun was shining in a brilliant blue sky and all was well with the world.

'Morning hinny,' said nana. 'It's a grand day fer the seaside.'

'It's champion nana,' agreed Alistair. 'I can't wait to get going.'

'Whey, will yer give bugger lugs up there another shout? An' mek sure he's up. Then sit yer sen at the table an' ar'll get yer cornflakes.'

'Are you up yet Roy?' called Alistair from the bottom of the stairs.

'Aye, divent panic, ar's on me way!' came Roy's reply, before muttering, 'He's too enthusiastic that bugger, ower excited Yorkshire berk. The goody two shoes is always downstairs first, mekking me look lazy – the creep. Ar'll be glad when he gans back home . . . It's never as hectic when he's not here, licking everyone's arse, fussing aboot like an old washer woman.'

'Good of you to put in an appearance,' said Roy's mother as he strolled into the dining room, yawning his head off.

'Whey, ar get a proper wash of a morning, unlike Yorky boy there. He won't need to go in the sea to get a tide mark round his neck, he's already got one.'

'I haven't got a tidemark, scrubbing brush head,' objected Alistair. 'I bet my neck's cleaner than yours.'

'Give it a rest ye two,' scolded nana. 'Ar divent want yer falling out an' carrying on, today of all days.'

'Sorry nana,' said Alistair.

'Aye, me too nana,' added Roy.

'Good, I don't want no bad feelings,' continued nana. 'It's to be a pleasurable outing, with nee bickering. Finish yer breakfasts an' then get yer sens ready while Kitty an' me finish mekking the sandwiches.'

'What's that smell?' remarked Roy, dropping his spoon in his bowl of cereal. "As somebody dropped one?'

'It's only the boiled eggs,' said nana. 'Ar've done yer two each. Do yer want to tek dandelion an' burdock or lemonade?'

'Dandelion an' burdock for me please nana.'

'Yer like that divent yer our Alistair?'

'Aye, it suits me fine,' he said getting up from the table. 'I'm just off to the toilet.'

'Don't ferget to get yer beach ball while yer up there,' taunted Roy. 'Yer nar why he's rushing to the bog divent yer?' he said when Alistair was out of earshot. 'Excitement . . . His arse cheeks'll be vibrating like a jack 'ammer.'

'Stop being so crude our Roy, or ar'll wash yer mouth out wi' soap an' watter,' scolded his mother,

'Well, I'm sorry mother, but it's true. Whenever he gets ower excited, he 'as to rush off to the toilet. Yer'll find that never 'appens with me . . . Ar's cool, calm an' collected. They divent call me the Stanhope rock fer nowt yer nar.'

'Yer just a thick skinned bugger ye. Nip upstairs will yer, an' get me a towel from the airing cupboard. Tek yer winkle pickers with yer an' all – yer nana poilshed 'em fer yer this morning.'

'Thanks nana!' he called through to the kitchen.

'Yer welcome pet!'

After delivering a towel to his mother, Roy sped back upstairs to find Alistair rummaging through a drawer. He took out his swimming trunks and put them on the bed.

''Ave yer got yer rubber duck out o' the bathroom?' skitted Roy.

'No clever clogs – I've borrowed yours from out o' the toy box Geordie.'

'Keep yer 'air on Yorky boy, ar's only joking man. 'Ave yer no sense o' humour?'

Roy went over to the wardrobe mirror. Striking a pose, he put on his sunglasses. He turned his head at different angles, trying to see his profile. 'Bah, ar's a handsome devil . . . Ar canna get ower me sen. Tek me looks fer granted at times I do. Ar divent nar how lucky I am. What's it like being ugly our kid?'

'You should know dreamer. I think there must be something wrong with your eyesight.'

'Well, you just observe the professional bird puller this afternoon . . . Watch and learn sonny boy . . .'

Chapter 5

Auntie Kitty locked the front door and placed the key on the skylight ledge above. Leaving your key without any worries of theft was normal practice. Burglars were unheard of in Stanhope in 1963.

Auntie Kitty carried a shopping bag containing the sandwiches and a flask of tea. Roy, to his dismay was ordered to carry the second shopping bag which was packed with towels and pop and all the other things neccessary for a day trip.

They passed Mrs Lister in her usual stance on the doorstep. Nana and Kitty gave a cursory nod, which she returned somewhat reluctantly.

'Mrs Lister not ganning on the trip then?' questioned Roy, a little further on down the Square. 'She'd be a right barrel o' laughs she would. She'd 'ave us rolling aboot in the bus aisle.'

'Stop being so facetious Roy!' reproached his mother. 'Admitted, the woman's an oddball, but she does nee harm to anyone, an' she keeps herself to herself . Have some respect fer yer elders.'

'Sorry mother, but she is strange all the same . . . '

Passing the town hall, they could hear singing in the distance.

'We're all ganning on a summer holiday
Nee more working for a week or two
Fun and laughter on our summer holiday
Nee more worries for me and you . . oo . . oo
For a week ot two.'

'Bloody hell!' exclaimed Roy. 'Ar didn't nar Cliff Richard was a Weardaler!'

'Language Roy!'

'Sorry nana . . . but ar hope that lot's not on our bus. Ar canna abide happy singing kids. They should come with a zip on their gobs so's us grown ups can travel in peace.'

'Divent be a misery guts. It wasn't so long ago that you were one o' them excited, happy little kids,' nana reminded him.

'Ar might 'ave been a bairn, but ar was never childish. Ar was always ahead of me time. I'm certain that if you study Einstein's family tree, yer'd find me amongst the branches somewhere.'

'You'd be the tree trunk more like,' muttered Alistair. 'Yer as thick as one.'

'Hey up, it's still alive! Ar thought you'd dropped off to sleep.'

'I'm wide awake, just can't get a word in edgeways 'cause your mouth never stops. I won't be long, I'm just nipping in the toilet.'

'What was ar saying aboot excited kids? His arse 'as never been away from the toilet all morning.'

'Stop being crude Roy. Ar want yer on yer best behaviour today lad.'

'Yes mother.'

Alistair rejoined the group and they carried on the rest of the short distance to the market place where the two coaches awaited them. Both coaches were already quite full. Some of the women remained outside gossiping whilst the drivers sat on a bench having a smoke and reading the morning papers.

'Oh no!' exclaimed Roy. 'It's them Haines brothers from Frosterley tekking us again. One's as deaf as a post, an' the other one, Mr MaGoo – he's as blind as a bat! We'll never get there in one piece.'

'Which one's which then?' asked Alistair.

'Whey, it's obvious Yorky boy. The one with the jam jar bottoms is the blind one, an' the one with the hearing trumpet is the deaf 'en.'

'Give ower exaggerating our Roy,' admonished Kitty. 'Both of 'em are steady drivers. At least they divent gan racing aboot like idiots.'

'Yer not wrong there mother. They tek aboot four hours to get to Whitley Bay. Ar could run there faster.'

'I wish you would,' grumbled Alistair. 'We'd 'ave a peaceful journey then.'

'Come on, yer'd miss my educating banter on the way, admit it.'

'Morning ladies,' greeted Alf, one of the coach drivers. 'I use the term loosely mind. 'Ave yer got a spare pair o' them bloomers with yer Molly, in case yer have a wet one?'

'Less of yer cheek, Frosterley lad, or ye'll be the wet one when ar drop yer in that sea.'

'Yer'll 'ave to catch me first Molly, an' ar canna see yer deeing that.'

'Nee problem. Our Kitty'll get 'old of yer. She's like a whippet our Kitty, once she gets ganning, isn't that right lass?'

'Aye, he's nee chance against me mother.'

'Whey so long as yer nar, yer up against the Frosterley one hundred yards champiom of 1936.'

'More like 1836,' whispered Roy to Alistair.

'Arraway with yer!' derided Molly. 'It's 1963 now, an' that beer belly'll slow yer right down.'

'What beer belly? That's just relaxed muscle man,' protested Alf, patting his stomach and trying to hold it in as best he could. 'Besides, ar divent drink beer or any other kind of alcohol fer that matter.'

'Eeh . . . yer lying bugger. Pull the other leg, it's got bells on. They call yer the Frosterley fish 'cause yer knock back that much ale.'

'Not me Molly,' Alf insisted. 'Ar think yer getting me mixed up with our Bert here.'

'That's not true Molly. Divent listen to a word he sez,' protested Bert. 'Ar's teetotal, ar can assure yer.'

'Another lying bugger! Yer both as bad as each other. Yer like two peas in a pod. Which bus are we on anyway?'

'Tek thee pick Molly,' said Alf. 'They're both ganning to the same place. Pass me yer hip flask out Bert . . . ar drive better wi' a drink inside me.'

The brothers laughed out loud together as Molly and Kitty looked on incredulously.

'Get on board Molly lass, we're just aving yer on,' Alf reassured her.

'Yer'll be having a clip round the ear if ar smell booze on any of yers.'

'As if we would. We'll be needing a couple o' pints tonight mind. After a day with ye lot carrying on, we'll 'ave earned it.'

Nana and Kitty sat together about halfway down the bus. Alistair and Roy sat directly behind them. Much to Roy's annoyance, the back seats were already taken. He liked being at the back, posing and waving at any girls they passed. Still, he thought, looking for some consolation, they kept the sick buckets at the back. He took comfort in knowing that he wouldn't have to sit inhaling the contents of them for hours on end.

'Where do they get these antique buses from?' remarked Alistair derisively.

'Whey, from Frosterley bus depot,' stated Roy. 'Why, what's up with 'em like?'

'I've seen better vehicles on Wagon Train. Our buses in Leeds are much more modern. These old things wouldn't be allowed on our roads. I mean, just look at the seats . . . The upholstery's made out of dinosaur hide.'

'Whey, if yer divent like it Yorky, yer can always bugger off back to Leeds an' ride round on yer modern buses. But just remember, yer've not got our oldie worldy buses and beautiful scenery – None of your concrete shite buildings up here boy.'

Alistair glanced at his Timex, 'Five past eight. I thought we were supposed to set off at eight.'

'They never set off on time man, ar telt yer the other day. Have some patience – besides, Stuart an' Billy 'aven't arrived yet. If they take much longer, these seats aside us'll be tekken.'

Roy was sitting next to the window and Alistair noticed how he continually looked at his reflection. To say he was vain would be the understatement of the century. If he were on his own, thought Alistair – he'd be kissing his reflection.

'Hey up!' exclaimed Roy. 'The lads are here!' He knocked excitedly on the window. 'Quick, get on board sharpish, there's empty seats beside us!'

'Not so loud Roy!' reprimanded his mother. 'It's like 'aving the town crier behind us. It's a good job yer nana's deaf,' she joked.

'Divent ye start our Kitty. There's nowt wrong wi' my lugs. Ar can hear a pin drop fifty yards away.'

'Ar'll back yer there nana,' said Roy. 'Yer can be in the kitchen an' me granda only 'as to rustle a ten bob note in the bedroom an' yer ears prick up.'

'Aye, nowt gets past me bonny lad. Ar nar all yer granda's hiding places an' all. Divent you let on to him mind.'

Billy and Stuart ambled down the coach aisle and sat themselves on the seat adjacent to the lads, their siblings and mothers sat in front of them.

'Alright chaps?' greeted Roy. 'Ar've not seen much of yer this holiday Stuart, where've yer been hiding yer sen?'

'Me favver's kept me busy on his milk round,' replied Stuart, yawning. 'Ar's up with the larks every morning, an' by the time ar's finished ar's knackered. Nee energy left to go gallavanting aboot. It's got it's compensations like . . . I've got a few bob stashed away in me post office account.'

Stuart, at five foot nine inches was slightly taller than Roy. His dark hair, which he combed back with lashings of Brylcreem, was in complete contrast to Roy's fine, short cut, almost blonde hair. Like Roy, he wore winkle pickers, but with denim jeans and a white shirt – his role model being Billy Fury. He walked about with his legs apart trying to look tough, but Roy wasn't impressed with Stuart's gait, often inquiring of him as to whether he'd shit himself. He wasn't happy-go-lucky like Roy, and any ribbing he got was taken to heart, putting him in a sombre mood for the rest of the day.

By a quarter past eight, the coach was full and the driver boarded the vehicle to a crescendo of cheers from the younger children. Roy tutted and then turned his attentions to the other three lads. 'Ar see we've got Mr MaGoo again. How that bugger an' his brother are allowed to drive, ar'll never nar.'

'Whey, they probably learned to drive in the army, an' didn't 'ave to pass a driving test. Things like that went on – according to me favver like,' said Stuart.

'We'll be half the day getting to Whitley Bay,' grumbled Roy. 'Both of 'em drive at a snails pace. Last year a tortoise overtook us – Hey up, Alf's getting back off the bus. He'll be going to crank their Bert's bus up, an' then Bert'll dee this one. Look at 'em, they're like a couple o' farts in a trance man. Talk aboot poetry in motion . . . Ar've seen more life in a tramps vest.'

Alf boarded the bus for the second time to resounding cheers from the kids. 'Right,' he said. 'Are we all ready to go to the seaside?'

'Yes . . . ' muttered Roy through gritted teeth. 'We've been ready fer the last half hour. They winna all be so enthusiastic when we break down. Mind you, they'll probably mek a big adventure out of it. It'll be us bigger lads that'll be the mugs pushing the bugger.'

'Will you stop moaning on Roy?' scolded his mother. 'It's two years since the bus broke down, an' then we were only delayed fer half an hour. The engine ower heated or summat, if ar recall.'

'What she means . . . ' explained Roy, 'Is that the shire horse pulling us, dropped dead.'

'What was that?'

'Nothing mother. Ar was just saying, ar was feeling a little hoarse. Ar'll 'ave a drink o' pop, soothe me throat like.'

To the excited cheers of the happy kids, the buses finally pulled out of the market place at twenty past eight.

'We're off at last,' sighed Billy.

The chorus struck up again, much to Roy's annoyance.

'We're all ganning on a summer holiday
Nee more working for a week or two . . . '

'Heaven help us,' he groaned, putting his hands over his ears. 'I'm definately not coming next year.'

''Ave we set off yet?' said Stuart sarcastically after they'd gone about half a mile.

'Course we 'ave,' said Billy. 'We're nearly up to ten mile an hour now.'

'Whey, wek me up when we get there,' said Stuart, closing his eyes and giving a contented sigh.

'Ar'll give yer a nudge in aboot five hours then,' said Billy obligingly.

'Why do they 'ave these blooming blowers?' grumbled Roy, fiddling with the knobs above his head. 'They never ruddy work.'

'Urgh! . . . Mammy, mammy, there's a hedgehog in front of me!' a youngster cried out.

'It's alright hinny, divent be scared, it's only Roy Osborne's heed,' his mother reassured him.

Roy turned round, putting on a false smile for the youngster, while at the same time making a V sign behind the seat so that he couldn't see.

Alistair and Billy chuckled as Roy turned to the front again, a sullen look on his face. He wasn't amused and was wondering which of the lads had put the youngster up to it. It would be pointless asking, because each one would blame the other. He leaned and whispered in Alistair's ear, 'When one o' them sick buckets is full, ar'll stick the little shits head in it.'

'Don't be rotten, yer miserable sod, he's only a bairn.'

'Whey, if he wants to grow up, he'd better leave my hair alone.'

The bottles of pop that had been generously donated by Stanhope Working Mens Club, had been handed round. Each bottle accompanied by a bag of crisps. All was peaceful for a short while as the youngsters tucked in – apart from the odd wail when someone couldn't find the little blue bag of salt.

Billy took charge of Stuart's pop and crisps because he was fast asleep. Working on his father's milk round every day had caught up with him, his body had shut down for a welcome respite. He even slept through a very loud, tuneless rendition of Living Doll.

'Is it true that when the cows lay down, it means it's going to rain?' asked Alistair.

'Nar . . . It means they're knackered,' came Roy's explanation.

'I should've known better than to ask you, prickhead.'

'Hey, watch it Olive Oyle . . . Billy, do you remember the other year when me nana bought a balloon fer our Alistair an' he started floating off? We grabbed his skinny little ankles just in time.'

'Aye, he was lucky mind,' said Billy, playing along with Roy.

Alistair didn't bother biting back. Once again, Roy had hit a raw nerve with him. He was very self concious about his stick insect build. How he envied other boys who had a bit of meat on them – they didn't know how lucky they were.

'Cheer up bonny lad,' said Roy. 'You look alright being slim . . . granda can use you as a pipe cleaner.'

Once again, Alistair didn't take the bait, he continued to look out of the window, ignoring Roy and Billy.

'Ooh . . . look Alistair, there's a bunny rabbit in that field – Isn't it cute?' teased Roy.

'Give it a rest big mouth!' snapped Alistair, resulting in the pair of them getting another telling off from auntie Kitty.

One or two children were wandering up and down the bus aisle. One particularly unruly lad whose mother rarely disciplined him – and on this occasion seemed to be turning a blind eye to him altogether – was going up to the other children and producing a frog from his pocket, causing shrieks of horror all around the bus. As he passed the lads Roy told him to **hop** it, or he'd end up with a **frog** in his throat. Even though Roy was only making a pathetic attempt at his repertoire of amphibian jokes, there was a sterness in his voice which had penetrated the child who returned to his seat, thus bringing the volume of screaming down to a more civilsed level.

'Bah, there's a stink! 'Ave you dropped one our Ali?'

'Not guilty Geordie, it's the little kiddies getting over excited. You used to drop 'em yourself not so long ago.'

'Who, me? Ar never did. Yer getting me mixed up wi' Billy.'

'What was that aboot me?'

'Our Alistair was just saying as to how ye used to fart a lot on the bus when yer got excited.'

'I didn't say that Billy!' Alistair protested. 'What I was saying was how it was Roy used to drop 'em in the past. You'll back me up won't you Billy?'

'Aye, yer right there. 'Ave yer seen his latest trick Ali?'

'What's that?'

'Whey, a few months back, we were round the playing field in the shelter like. Roy was farting an' holding a lighted match to his arse. Yer should 'ave seen it . . . Like a flame thrower it was. The wooden benches were scorched.'

'Divent exaggerate, they weren't scorched. It was good fun mind,' chuckled Roy. 'Very useful in winter – It warms the shelter up champion.'

'Yer went too far one day though . . . Do yer remember? Yer lit a rasper an' had to stick yer arse in the paddling pool to put the flames out.'

'Divent believe him Ali, he's telling a pack o' lies.'

'Billy wouldn't lie,' said Alistair stirring it, trying to get back at Roy.

'Will ye lot stop talking about breaking wind and other crudities,' reprimanded Kitty. 'Change the subject.'

Roy thought his mother was putting on airs and graces, but didn't say anything. Farts were allowed at home. In fact, one of his mother's favourite sayings was, 'Whose let off and never let on.'

The coach slowed down to a snails pace, bringing moans and groans from the passengers. Alf informed them that a tractor in front of Bert's coach was responsible for their slow progress, and that they would overtake when it was possible.

'Might as well nip out fer a slash,' skitted Roy. 'Bah! There's a right stink! Either someone's got the boiled eggs out or our Alistair's shit 'im sen.'

'Roy, that's enough! Behave yer sen!'

'Sorry mother.'

Eventually, both the coaches increased in speed as the tractor turned off up a muck road. Loud cheers ensued from the passengers. Several minutes later the coach went over a humped bridge which brought whoops of delight from the children as their stomachs lurched and left their bearings. Unfortunately for a couple of them, this caused adverse effects and the sick buckets at the back of the bus were sought out.

Roy was sitting with a wry smile on his face, enjoying every moment. 'Bah, that brings back memories . . . Alistair, nip to the back of the bus an' 'ave a gander in the sick bucket. Ar'll bet yer any money – there'll be carrots in it. The kids won't 'ave eaten any fer a month, but ar guarantee that bucket'll contain bits o' carrot.'

One of the mothers made her way to the front of the bus to ask Alf how long it would be before they had a toilet stop, because her little Jimmy couldn't hold on much longer. He assured her that they'd be pulling up at their regular toilet stop within the next few minutes. He also reminded her that they'd already be there, if they hadn't been delayed by the tractor.

True to his word, in no time at all, Alf pulled in alongside the public conveniences. 'Five minutes please and nee longer!' he announced. 'The sooner you're back on board, the sooner we get to Whitley Bay!'

Caught in the stampede, he regretted his last statement. 'Steady on, there's no need to break yer necks, we're not in that much of a rush!'

Stuart woke up, stretching and yawning. 'Are we there?' he asked.

'What d'yer mean?' said Roy mischievously. 'We're on our way home. You've slept through it.'

'Ar should be so lucky,' he murmured, closing his eyes again.

'Whey, if yer want a slash, yer'd better hurry up, we'll be setting off again in a minute.'

'Nar, ar divent need to gan.'

Nana and Kitty returned to their seats having availed themselves of the facilities. They enjoyed a couple of minutes peace and quiet before battle would recommence. These infrequent moments of calm had to be savoured because they were short lived. The imminent approach of the coastline would bring forth another crescendo of noise and the inevitable smells from the children.

Nana passed the boys a boiled egg each as Billy rummaged in his haversack and pulled out an apple before crunching into it with a lot of noise and relish. Stuart drank a bottle of milk – one of the perks of working on his father's milkround. He knew the milk was fresh – none of the day old stuff for him . . . that would be palmed off onto unsuspecting customers.

'Bah . . . them eggs stink, are they rotten?' complained Stuart.

'There's nowt wrong wi' them eggs young man,' stated nana indignantly. 'Fresh from granda's hens – unlike the one's ye sell.'

'Whey, ar divent think they smell ower much,' said Roy, adding his two pennorth. 'The smell mingles in with the little farties.'

'Are we all on board?' shouted Alf, walking down the bus aisle, making a head count.

'Yeah . . . !' screamed the kids, not really knowing or caring whether anyone was left behind.

Alf cranked Bert's bus up, who in turn did the same to his, and off they went to the usual resounding cheers.

''Ave yer seen that?' remarked Roy pointing out of the window. 'That's the second cyclist to overtake us this morning. We'd 'ave got there quicker on Billy's bogey.'

'I 'aven't 'ad a bogey fer years,' said Billy. 'Ar nar what yer mean though . . . I saw a bloke running past us not so long back.'

'Stop yer moaning ye lot,' chided Kitty. 'We've not far to gan now.'

Another few miles and the sea appeared on the horizon bringing an excited 'Hooray . . . !' followed by an out of tune rendition of 'I do like to be beside the seaside.'

'God help us,' pleaded Roy. 'Thank heavens we'll be getting off this travelling shit house soon.'

'Language Roy!' chastised his mother.

'Sorry, but it stinks . . . '

Chapter 6

Alf pulled up the coach directly behind his brother's in their usual parking spot right on the sea front. 'Okay everybody, listen up please! Be back here by six o'clock sharp and nee later mind or yer'll get left behind. Right, lecture ower with, all that's left fer me to say is have a great day everybody, an' see yer later!'

Kids were tripping over each other in the fight to exit the bus. Many getting a scolding or even a clip round the ear from their mothers. Nana, Kitty and the boys remained in their seats waiting for the stampede to subside.

They finally alighted from the bus, stepping out into the sunshine, Alf giving the ladies a helping hand.

'Watch where Mr MaGoo's putting his hands,' muttered Roy to the lads. 'We only managed to get here because Bert kept flashing a lantern in the back window of the bus. If a cop car or ambulance 'ad passed, Alf would've followed it.'

'Right lads,' said Kitty. 'We'll see yer back here at a quarter to six an' nee later mind – think on.'

'Stick together an' all,' added nana. 'Nee gallavanting off on yer own. Are yer listening Roy?'

'Yes nana, divent worry, ar'll look after little Alistair an' mek sure he gets his rusks an' milk on time. Ar've got his nappies an' 'is dummy etc.'

'Stop being so facetious Roy.'

'Sorry nana. You an' me mother get yer sens off to the bingo an' enjoy yer sens. If yer win owt, ar'll 'ave a new pair o' winkle pickers.'

'Aye, an' pigs might fly. Cheerio then.'

'See yer later!' echoed the lads as they set off down the promenade in the opposite direction.

Alistair was seething over Roy's infantile remarks, but kept quiet, thus depriving Roy of any smug satisfaction achieved from his retort.

The promenade and beach were beginning to get busy, the warm sun luring day trippers to the seaside like a giant magnet.

The boys passed a number of motor bikes parked by the roadside. Stuart examined them closely, admiring the different makes and the pristeen condition of them. The owners of the bikes – rockers, weren't far away. They were sitting on the beach, lads and lasses together, chatting and laughing, smoking and drinking beer straight from the bottle. They didn't seem to have a care in the world.

Roy turned and shouted after Stuart, 'Yer'd better get a move on! Yer divent want to hang aboot those bikes too long,' he advised. 'They might think yer tampering with 'em, or after stealing one an' then you'll get a good kicking. The last thing yer want is to mess with them. They'll be getting primed up, ready to tek on the mods later . . . You mark my words.'

As if on cue, a convoy of motor scooters passed the lads. This brought a barrage of jeers and threats from the direction of the beach. V signs and other offensive gestures were exchanged between both groups.

'There's nee love lost there,' commented Roy. 'It's all building up towards a ruction this afternoon, that's fer sure.'

'Will they be fighting an' carrying on in the amusement park then?' worried Alistair. 'They'll spoil it for everyone if they do.'

'Divent sweat on that score bonny lad,' Roy reassured him. 'The police winna let 'em near the Spanish City. Any battling between the mods an' rockers'll tek place on the beach. The police'll let 'em knock seven bells of shit out of each other, an' then step in an' mek a load of arrests.'

'You seem well informed aboot it all. How come?' quizzed Billy.

'Whey, ar've read all aboot it in the Norhtern Echo. All summer there's been mods versus rocker battles at all the other seaside towns. Redcar, Scarborough, Bridlington, down south . . . Ar could go on, it's rife man.'

Stuart stopped in his tracks as the smell of fried onions drifted towards them. 'Bah, that smells champion,' he said rubbing his hands together. 'Ar's getting me sen a hotdog, ar divent nar aboot ye lot.'

They all agreed, the smell from the hotdog stand was too good to pass without a purchase.

After getting served, they continued along the promenade, munching away on the long bread buns, smothered in tomato sauce and onions.

Naturally, Roy had cause for complaint. 'Whey, ar divent call this a hotdog! 'Ave yer seen the size of this bugger? Our Alistair's pecker's bigger than this excuse fer a sausage – an' that's only half an inch long!'

Billy and Stuart chuckled quietly, trying to suppress a laugh, while Alistair, nearly choking on his hotdog snapped, 'At least ar've got one, yer big girl!'

'Ooh . . . touched a nerve have we bonny lad?'

'Bollocks! You'll get your come uppance, just wait an' see.'

A couple of minutes silence ensued as the boys finished eating.

'Ar wonder why old ladies sit in deckchairs with their legs wide apart,' remarked Billy as they strolled along.

'Because it keeps the flies off their ice cream,' stated Roy casually.

The lads burst out laughing. Even Alistair couldn't hold back his mirth, though he did try.

'Ar must admit, after all these years of listening to your abysmal jokes, yer've actually cracked a funny one,' laughed Billy.

'Aye, ar'll not argue wi' that like,' added Stuart.

They all turned to Alistair, awaiting his comments. He didn't want to, but felt obliged to say something . . . and it might avert all the eyes boring into him. 'It wasn't bad,' he murmured, 'For a moron.'

'You have excellent taste gentlemen. Ar thought it was brilliant me sen,' boasted Roy.

The Spanish City amusement park came into view. In complete contrast to last years wash out, the main entrance was bustling, much to Roy's delight. His face was lit up like a Christmas tree.

'If ar divent pull a bird today, I'll show my arse in Burton's window.'

'Well, that's summat to look forward to,' sneered Alistair. 'I can't wait. Yer talk through it all the time – we might as well see it.'

'Nee chance o' that Yorky boy, the lasses'll be all ower me . . . like bees round a honey pot.'

The other lads looked at each other, not passing comment, choosing not to add further fuel to the fire.

Bobby Vee's, The Night Has a Thousand Eyes blared from the direction of the waltzers as they entered The Spanish City.

All the lads had an adrenaline rush, excitement oozing from every pore. Each of them tried not to show their own excitement to their fellow companions – that wouldn't be cool.

'Stuart . . . ' said Roy.

'Yes?'

'What time do yer have to be home tonight?'

'Same time as everyone else. That's a daft question – What d'yer want to nar that for?'

'Whey, ar was just wondering what time yer mam an' dad were ganna fry their fish an' chips, come tea-time. With you 'aving all the lard on yer heed like.'

'That's rich coming from ye, cactus heed. My greased back rocker style haircut is all the rage man. Your crew cut is way out of date.'

Stuart waited for the onslaught of verbal abuse to follow, and true to form, Roy didn't disappoint.

'Whey, if you're a rocker – chip fat heed – why divent yer gan an' join 'em on the beach then? It's because yer'd bore 'em to death. What would yer talk aboot? How to deliver a pint of sour milk in three easy lessons? Or would yer tek 'em some milk an' eggs an' cook 'em a Hells Angel omelette fer breakfast? Or mebbe slit a live chicken's throat an' drink its blood fer yer initiation ceremony before yer . . . '

'Alright, alright, divent gan overboard! I only said yer crew cut was out of date.'

'Ar'll show yer who's got the best haircut. All your dreams are realised girls . . . The Stanhope Stud is back in town.'

Plenty of girls, mostly in groups of three and four, were standing beside the various rides. They stood listening to the latest records while eyeing up the best looking lads.

Roy was in his element, strutting about, wolf whistling at any fanciable female. Any smile or wave he received in return, he would stick out his chest, making himself look even more like a peacock. 'Ar telt yer boys, they're gagging fer it. 'Ave yer seen 'em all eyeing me up? Come on, let's chat them four up, aside the waltzers.'

The boys followed Roy up the steps, Alistair with butterflies in his stomach. Stuart was a little apprehensive, while Billy was completely unfazed. Like Roy, he didn't give a monkeys uncle. Trying to appear casual, they leaned themselves against the wooden bannister next to the girls.

Roy broke the ice, 'Are yer alright ladies?'

They smiled nervously and one of them answered, 'Not bad, are you?'

'I am now ar've met four gorgeous girls. Where yer from like?'

'Leeds,' they chorused.

'That's a coincidence, our Alistair's from Leeds, aren't yer boy?'

'Yes,' replied Alistair, blushing, looking at his feet.

'He's shy. He usually gans on the beach an' builds sandcastles with his nana an' auntie Kitty, but this year they've let him loose with the big boys.'

'Or . . . leave him alone,' said the girl who spoke before. 'I think he's cute. Are the rest of you Geordies then?'

'No bonny lass, we're Weardalers,' corrected Roy.

'What's one o' them?'

'Whey, 'ave yer heard o' Bishop Auckland?'

'Yes.'

'Well we live aboot twenty miles on from there, in a Weardale village called Stanhope – hence we're called Weardalers. What are yer names girls anyway?'

The same girl did the introductions, 'I'm Karen, I'm eighteen. This is Sarah, she's seventeen and these two here are sisters. Laura's sixteen and Katy's the youngest – she's fourteen. We call her Ken because she's a tomboy.'

'Go on, tell the world,' objected Katy. 'An' get it right, I **used** to be a tomboy.'

'Well, I'm only telling the truth,' insisted Karen. 'Your turn now lads, introduce yerselves.'

Naturally, Roy was spokesman. 'Whey, I'm Roy, the eldest and best looking as you can see. Ar's sixteen,' he lied, without batting an eyelid. 'This is my workmate Stuart, an' he's the same age as me. Billy here, he's fifteen. We call him carrot top for obvious reasons . . . '

'Divent start,' interrupted Billy. 'Ar divent nar how yer've got the cheek, the state o' your heed!'

'Now, now boys, calm down,' said Sarah. 'Yer on a day trip an' supposed to be enjoying yerselves. You can bicker when yer get home.'

'Aye, yer right,' agreed Roy. 'Ar'll finish me introductions. This is our Alistair. Like ar said, he's from Leeds an' he's staying wi' me to be educated and cultured. Oh – an' he'll be nine next birthday.'

'I don't believe that for one minute,' said Laura. 'How old are you Alistair?'

'I'm twelve,' he stated shyly. 'But I'm more grown up than my big headed cousin!'

'Yeah, I can believe that.'

'Rubbish!' scoffed Roy. 'They divent call me the Stanhope professor fer nowt yer nar.'

'Is he always so full of himself?' asked Karen.

'Ar nar what he is full of,' stated Billy. 'But ar winna repeat it in front of you ladies.'

'Creep,' muttered Roy.

'I think we know what you mean, don't we girls?'

Roy changed the subject and crossing his fingers behind his back asked, 'Do you fancy a walk round the amusements with us?'

'It was with some relief when Karen answered. 'I don't see why not, do you girls? It should be a laugh if nothing else.'

'Great! This way girls.' Roy spread out his arms, inviting them to proceed ahead. 'We're right behind you.'

Roy was in his element, strutting around the amusement park with four lasses in tow. He was up at the front amongst them, his gob going ten to the dozen, while the other lads kept their distance behind.

'These lasses winna hang aboot with us fer long,' muttered Billy. 'He's boring 'em to death. Just look at their faces . . . They're pissed off. Ar'd better gan an' rescue 'em.'

Billy stepped up his pace to join the group in front, Stuart wasn't far behind. Alistair bringing up the rear, not very comfortable in the presence of strangers, especially female ones.

'Are yer in Whitley Bay fer a while, or just on a day trip like us?' asked Billy.

'A day trip, same as you,' replied Laura.

'Let's go in there!' enthused Katy, spotting the hall of mirrors. 'It should be a laugh.'

'Whey, ar's game,' said Billy. 'How aboot you lads? Hang on a minute though . . . Roy canna gan in. He got barred last year – his ugly mug cracked all the mirrors!'

The girls all laughed, much to Roy's annoyance.

'That's very funny carrot top. Yer a barrel o' laughs, ar don't think.'

After paying at the turnstile, they first went through a short corridor of mirrors. They laughed at their distorted reflections before arriving in a larger round room, filled from floor to ceiling with mirrors. They had the room completely to themselves, and all inhibitions evaporated as they collapsed into fits of uncontrollable giggles.

'Hey! Look at this one!' exclaimed Roy. 'Even our Alistair's got some meat on him!' he laughed.

'At least I can fit fully on,' retorted Alisatir. 'Even the widest mirror wouldn't be able to squeeze your head on.'

'Ar look seven feet tall in this one!' exclaimed Stuart.

'Whey, when yer've finished looking in that one, let our Alistair 'ave a go. He can lob 'is tiny pecker out. It should mek it twice as long, a full inch!'

'Stop showing off, hedgehog head. At least I don't talk like a prick.'

'You tell him!' encouraged Karen. 'He's too big for his boots is your cousin.'

'Yeah, stop being such a bully,' added Sarah.

'Alright, alright, keep yer 'air on girls. Ar was only 'aving a bit of a joke like. Divent you 'ave a sense o' humour in Yorkshire?'

'Course we do,' said Karen. 'The difference being, is your defenition of a sense of humour is a nasty one. Picking on people all the time isn't funny. You're supposed to laugh with people, not at them. You won't win any friends acting like a pillock all yer life.'

Roy was dumbstruck. It wasn't often anyone spoke so forcefully about him to his face, least of all a girl. Still, it would soon be water off a ducks back. He was too thick skinned for it to prey on his mind for too long. The girls remarks would exit his empty head as quickly as they had entered it.

The other lads had looked at one another in smug satisfaction, no further comment neccessary.

'Right, I've had enough mirrors for one day,' declared Laura. 'If yer've all finished looking at yerselves, let's get ganning – I mean going.' She made for the exit, the rest of the group in close pursuit.

A short stroll preceded a stop at the bumping cars. They climbed the wooden steps onto the platform that surrounded the circuit. 'Let's Dance,' blared from the speakers, one of which was set directly above their heads. They watched as the cars set off. A scruffy looking fairground worker would jump on the back of each car, holding onto the pole that sparked overhead. Extending his other arm to the front of the car, he would wait for the occupant's fare to be placed in his greasy palm.

'A good bath wouldn't gan amiss wi' some o' them mucky buggers,' proclaimed Roy, his mouth back in motion. 'They even mek ye look smart Stuart, an' that's saying summat. Now they **are** yer proper greasers,' he stated.

'Whey, most of 'em'll be on the run from the pollace, or fiddling the dole,' added Billy. 'They divent get paid ower much, so they try an' short change yer. All the scrubbers hang round 'em. Some of 'em gan back to their wagons or caravans after the rides are shut down an' get a good seeing to.'

'You're well informed Billy,' remarked Karen. 'Did you used to work on the fair?'

'Me? No, never. We 'ave an annual agricultural show back in Stanhope an we 'ave a fair down the main street. Yer get to nar one or two of the fair lads. There is a few of 'em that are 'alf decent mind, an' they're the ones that tell yer all the goings on. If ar went into too much detail, ar'd mek you ladies blush.'

'Don't hold back on account of us,' said Laura. 'We're from the city don't forget, an' probably seen a lot more of life than you young lads.'

'That's as maybe, but ar's saying nee more.'

'Spoilsport!'

'Stuart's ganning to work on the fair,' announced Roy. 'Another eighth of an inch of lard on his heed an' he'll get tekken on.'

'Listen who's talking,' derided Stuart who, normally a placid lad, wasn't going to be made a fool of in front of the girls, especially as he'd taken a shine to Laura. 'At least ar don't stink o' Turners farm permanently. Ar'd 'ave thought ye an ideal candidate fer a fairground lad.'

'Bollocks! Excuse my French ladies, but ar always have a bath or a good wash when ar've been farming . . . unlike ye Regent. Ye smell o' sour milk an' Brylcreem, yer big greaseball.'

Alistair, diplomatically interrupted the bickering. 'I'm off to the toilet, anyone coming?'

'Aye, ar'll join yer an' gan fer a smoke,' said Roy. 'If ar light up here, someone from the coach might see me an' tell me mother.'

'So what? You're sixteen an' old enough to smoke aren't you?' questioned Karen.

Roy, realising what he'd said, stuttered awkwardly. 'Wh . . . whey, ar's old enough like, but me mother still prefers me not to smoke.' He groaned inwardly to himself and hastily followed Alistair.

'How do you put up with that Roy?' asked Katy. 'He'd drive me round the bend.'

The other girls nodded in agreement.

'Whey ar divent see much of him in the holidays,' sighed Stuart. 'I'm always working on me favver's milkround. We see more of each other at school . . . Whey – what ar mean is, we used to see more of each other before we left school.'

'I thought you two worked together,' commented Laura looking slightly puzzled.

'Up until recently we did,' said Stuart, thinking fast. 'Ar left farming to work full time on me favver's milk round.'

'You had a lucky escape then,' she smiled.

'Whey, ar wouldn't say that. Yer do get used to him after a while. Ar nar he's ower loud an' big headed, but tek away the outer shell . . . an' there's still a pillock inside. Nar . . . I'm only joking. Underneath, he's not a bad lad.'

'That's as maybe, but if he carried on like that in front of the lads that I know back in Leeds, he'd end up with a thick ear.'

'He's well known yer see in Stanhope. People tek 'im wi' a pinch o' salt – most of 'em anyway. It's when yer gan somewhere where yer not known. His big mouth can get yer in trouble then. He doesn't usually push it too far. He's not daft yer nar, he just acts it.'

The bumping cars stopped.

'Do yer fancy coming on with me Laura?' Stuart asked. 'Ar's paying,' he quickly added.

'Whey, ar canna refuse an offer like that bonny lad,' replied Laura in her best Weardale accent.

'Reet lass. I'm glad tha's said yes,' said Stuart, not to be outdone in the dialect department.

Billy was left alone with the other girls, but was not fazed in the slightest. 'How's aboot one of you lasses ganning on the next ride with me?'

'I'll go with you,' volunteered Sarah, before the other two had a chance to open their mouths.

'Yer on. Ar'll grab a car when they stop . . . Stay in that car!' he shouted to Stuart and Laura as they passed on their way round. Stuart gave him the thumbs up. Saving the car for them meant they wouldn't have to battle through a frenzied mob at the end of the ride.

Roy was standing in the toilet puffing away on a cigarette, blowing smoke rings into the air. He banged on a cubicle door. 'Ha way man! Them Leeds birds'll be wondering where ar've got to. What yer deeing in there, 'aving a wank? Yer dirty little git!'

'No, I'm not!' protested Alistair. 'Bog off if yer in such a hurry.'

'Nar . . . Ar'll hang on fer yer in case yer get lost on the way back. Ar'd be in fer a bollocking off me mother if ar lost yer. Wipe yer arse an' let's get ganning – My female admirers await my return.'

They set off to make their way back to the others, declining offers on the way to throw darts or shoot airgun pellets at a target. Even 'hook a duck' didn't tempt them.

'Bleeding goldfish,' chuntered Roy. 'How many times 'ave we won one at Stanhope show, our kid? They all dee on yer. Ar think the longest time one lived was fer four days. A waste o' time man.'

'Well, yer not supposed to put 'em in hot water yer know,' admonished Alistair.

'Divent exaggerate. Ar tried tepid watter once, but it made no difference. They all kicked the bucket whatever we tried.'

Passing the kiddies roundabout, they overheard a little girl, 'Mummy, look! Is that one o' them misters from the circus?'

'Where pet? I don't know who yer mean.'

'That man there mummy . . . Look! He's got a clown's shoes on!' she shrieked, pointing at Roy.

'No hinny, that's not a clown. It's just a lad wi' shoes on that look a bit like a clowns.'

'Little shit,' muttered Roy, increasing his pace.

'Don't be miserable,' said Alistair, laughing. 'The little kid doesn't know any better. Anyway, you must admit, yer winkle pickers are turning up at the ends, yer've had 'em that long.'

'Whey, why is it, it's always me that's the source of fun? Tell me that Yorky boy.'

'Now yer getting paranoid.'

'Rubbish!'

Passing the speedway, Roy stopped in his tracks. 'Bah! Look at that our kid!' he exclaimed, pointing to a short skirted blonde standing on the wooden steps. 'She's gorgeous! Ar tell yer what kidder . . . Ar'd use her shit fer toothpaste.'

'Urgh! that's the worst yer've come out with yet. What an awful expression. I knew you could be crude, but that's awful!'

'Ah . . . stop being a prude all yer life. 'Ave a day off fer once. Just look at them legs . . . beautiful or what?'

'Stop trying to see up her skirt, yer pervert.'

'It's only natural man. Why aren't you 'aving a butchers anyway? Are yer a puff or summat? Ar've got me doubts aboot ye lad. Ar think yer'll 'ave to stop kipping in my bed. Ar divent want nee woolly woofter interfering with me when ar's asleep . . . Waking up with a little Yorkshire pecker sticking in me back.'

'Do you know? You're a mentalist!' retorted Alistair. 'You want locking up in the looney bin.'

A young man carrying a stick of candyfloss walked up to the girl Roy had been ogling, and they walked off together hand in hand.

'Orh . . . How unlucky can that lass get? Ar was just aboot to chat her up an' all.'

'Ha ha, you're too late Geordie boy, she's spoken for. You wouldn't 'ave 'ad a chance anyway.'

'Ah well, nee good crying ower spilt milk. Let's get back an' join your fellow countrymen, or women in this case.'

'Fellow **county** women, don't you mean?'

'Whatever . . . Eeh by gum. What's tha' splitting hairs for? Can thee ride a tandem?'

'They're from Yorkshire, not Wales!' derided Alistair at Roy's attempt of his native tongue.

'Bah, yer a miserable sod. Lighten up bonny lad. Tell yer what, sing us that daft Yorkshire song . . . How's it gan? Where 'as tha' bin since ar saw thee . . . On tilk lee moor bar tadpole. What's all that shite aboot like?'

'Well if yer sang the right words it might help, yer moron. It goes like this . . . ' Alistair cleared his throat. 'Where 'as tha' been since ar saw thee . . . On Ilkley moor ba' t' hat . . . Where 'as tha' been since ar saw thee . . . and so on.'

'It's still a load o' bollocks,' insisted Roy.

'Yeah, I must admit it's a weird little ditty,' agreed Alistair. 'It's all gobbledygook to me, an' probably to all other Yorkshire folk an' all.'

'I always said that ye lot were odd. What with all yer daft sayings, an' yer whippets an' flat caps.'

'They're just myths. Nobody in our family wears flat caps – an' we certainly don't keep whippets. You've some brass neck anyway, calling Yorkshire folk odd. At least we don't serve cow pats on our plates – what you lot call pease pudding – fer some obscure reason. We also have half a dozen picture houses within a mile of our house. We don't 'ave to go to the local town hall to see films. You 'ave to sit on tablets of stone an' the usherette walks around in roman sandals. Talk about Stonehenge being out of date. Stanhope meks them boulders look brand new.'

'Whey, yer nar what to dee if yer divent like it – bog off back to your so called modern city!' retorted Roy.

Alistair chose not to defend his home town. He continued to stroll along with Roy, making his tongue in cheek comments, criticising Stanhope, putting down his own most favourite place in the whole world.

His tirade had served it's purpose into stirring Roy into his usual onslaught of verbal abuse. If the truth be known though, Alistair much preferred watching films in Stanhope town hall than in any of the picture houses back home in Leeds. Anything connected with the idyllic Weardale village was alright by him – but why tell Roy and spoil the fun?

Billy and Sarah were climbing out of a bumping car as Alistair and Roy rejoined the group.

'Hey up! You lucky girls, ar's back. Did yer miss me?' called Roy, brash as ever as he approached them.

'Like we missed the plague,' muttered Laura.

'Ye took yer time,' commented Stuart. 'Did the pollace pick yer up fer vagrancy?' Stuart was feeling a little cocky now he'd been on the bumping cars with Laura, who happened to be standing by his side right now.

'You've come out of yer shell all of a sudden milky boy. Divent ye get above yer station. If yer must nar, ar had to wait fer our Alistair to finish playing with him sen. Then, on the way back, all the birds kept stopping me an' chatting me up.'

'Stop lying,' said Alistair blushing.

'Don't worry love,' Karen reassured him. 'We don't believe him for one moment.'

The bumping cars came to a halt once again. Before you could say Jack Robinson, Roy was scrambling into a car parked in the middle of half a dozen by the track side. His face was a picture with a satisfied smirk right across it, so full of himself. He failed to notice that the surrounding cars around him were empty.

'Heh heh, watch this!' chortled Billy.

The siren went off, signalling the start of the next ride. Roy's car didn't move an inch. As he pressed the pedal frantically, he realised now why the surrounding cars were empty. He'd only gone and jumped into a dud one.

The thought that this possibly wasn't going to be his day went through his head, as he reluctantly slouched back to his companions, his tail between his legs. That thought would soon evaporate though, being the positive, thick skinned person he was. He approached the group with apprehension, bracing himself in readiness for their gleeful derision.

Stuart and Billy were doubled up over the wooden bannister, laughing through to their boots. Alistair and the girls weren't so blatant in their mockery, but there was no mistaking the mirth on their faces. Yes, Roy's embarrassment had brought untold joy to all.

'Eeh look, he's blushing,' said Billy, finally bringing himself to an upright position. 'Now, that is one for the record books. Ar've never, ever seen Roy gan red.'

'Yer set of twats!' fumed Roy. 'Yer could've telt me them cars were out of action!'

'Whey, we didn't even nar yer'd gone,' said Billy, trying to stifle another bout of laughter. 'We looked round and there yer were – sat in the car with a stupid grin on yer face. Besides, why should we spoil our fun?'

'Where's Katy gone to?' asked Sarah, looking round.

'On the slot machines, more than likely,' tutted Laura. 'She's a bit of a gambler is our Ken. A couple of years ago when we were on holiday in Blackpool, she went missing . . . Well, what I mean is, she didn't come back to the hotel when she should've done. We didn't panic though. The hotel we stay at is right opposite the south pier, which just happens to be full of slot machines. We went over and sure enough, there she was, her pockets bulging with change. Even if she's not winning any money, our Ken's got an uncanny knack of finding it. She's dead jammy that way.'

The amusement park was bustling, getting busier by the minute. When the bumping cars came to a halt, Roy didn't attempt to secure one this time, using the excuse that it was getting too busy. What he really meant was he didn't want to be shown up again. Composure was the order of the day. Just for the time being . . .

Katy reappeared.

'Where've yer been? As if I need to ask,' said Laura.

'I had to rush to the toilet,' Katy claimed, not very convincingly.

'Well, did yer win owt?'

'Can't complain,' she grinned, rattling the change in her pocket.

'Did you get it legally, or illegally?'

'Both really. I got three cherries worth one an' sixpence, an' it didn't pay out, so I gave it a good shake an' it dropped three shillings!'

'Didn't anyone see you?'

'Not as far as I know. They wouldn't 'ave 'eard owt, the music was too loud.'

'Yer've more jam than Hartleys,' said Sarah. 'Whenever we pass a phone box yer know, Ken nips in, presses button B, an' nine times out of ten, it drops some coins.'

'Don't exaggerate Sarah. It's not that often I find money – an' stop calling me Ken.'

'I don't know about you lot, but I fancy an ice cream or summat,' said Karen.

'Ooh yeah, so do I,' agreed Sarah. 'Is anyone else coming?'

With the weather being so good, there was a bit of a queue at the ice cream kiosk. They waited patiently and chatted away like old friends, the atmosphere between them was now much more relaxed

Roy stuck his knee into the back of Alistair's causing his legs to buckle.

'Give over yer big kid! Can't you stand still an' act normal just for one minute?' he snapped.

'Whey, if normal means being like ye, ar divent want nowt to dee with it. Lighten up boy. Ar've telt yer afore – Relax, let yer sen gan. Go on . . . buy yer sen a cider lolly. On second thoughts, divent dee that. The last time you 'ad one o' them, I ended up carrying yer home.'

'Don't lie. Anyway, you've got a cheek. 'Ave you forgotten last spring? That bloke, John Bickers, he came round the shelter an' you helped him drink a bottle o' cider. For ten minutes you staggered about, an' then ran into the toilets an' spewed yer ring up.'

'Alright Yorky boy, yer divent 'ave to tell the world. I was only sick because the cider was off.'

'If that were true, how come John wasn't ill? He drank the same cider.'

'Whey man, he's got guts o' steel. He drinks like a fish. Rumour has it he even drinks meths. Aye, he's an alcoholic is John . . . He's twenty two years old an' never worked. They say his last job was school prefect.'

'Is that the only joke yer nar?' groaned Billy. 'Ar must've heard it a dozen times.'

'Whey, at least ar have a go. We divent hear ye tellng any.'

'That's because ar winna mek a prat of me sen, unlike ye.'

'Bollocks! Yer just like out Alistair, a miserable git.'

Chapter 7

'House!'

'Bloody hell!' exclaimed Kitty in disgust. 'That's four games out of the last eight, she's won – the hussy.'

Molly and Kitty had been playing prize bingo on the sea front for the past two hours, with limited success.

'Ar've seen that bingo caller ogling her all the time,' skitted Molly. 'He's not very discreet aboot it neither,' she tutted. 'They've got some fiddle going on between them, it's obvious. He'll be getting his favours returned after he's finished here.'

'Eeh, mother! Yer getting a cynical bugger in yer old age,' chuckled Kitty.

'Whey, ar mean – it's as plain as the nose on yer face. Ar tell yer what our Kitty, we'll gan somewhere else to play bingo next year. Let's mek this our last game. Ar could do wi' stretching me legs an' a nice pot o' tea. Mind you, a cuppa winna quench me thirst this weather – we'll 'ave something cooler.'

'Suits me mother, ar's parched. How many vouchers 'ave we won?'

'Let's see . . . Five. Not many fer all that brass we've spent,' sighed Molly.

They played their last game and the young woman won again. Molly was incensed and couldn't contain herself any longer. 'It's a bloody fix!' she shouted. 'That's five of the last nine games she's won! You canna tell me yer not fiddling!'

'I assure you madam, it's all down to luck,' insisted the caller. 'It all depends on how the balls come out.'

'Aye, an' it'll be your balls coming out tonight, an' she'll be playing with 'em, yer bent bugger!'

The other bingo players were in hysterics, thoroughly enjoying this diversion. All the poor girl could do was look at the floor, her face scarlet with embarrassment. There was no way she could tackle the full verbal onslaught from this angry woman.

Even the bingo caller was red as a beetroot. Sweating profusely, he loosened his collar, coughed, and cleared his throat before hastily going on to the next game. 'Eyes down for your next house.'

'Calm down mother, yer'll be having one of yer funny turns,' chortled Kitty.

'Whey, the brazen monkey. Ar've a good mind to give 'im a thick ear.'

'Ha way mother, let's swop our vouchers,' said Kitty, leading Molly towards the end of the counter where the prizes were displayed on the shelves.

A miserable young female assistant took the vouchers from them, and then pointed out the merchadise available with the five wins.

'Not much bloody choice is there?'

'Stop cursing mother, settle down.'

'Whey, there isn't is there? What do you fancy our Kitty?'

'Whey, let's see . . . there's a butter dish . . .'

'We've got one.'

'Okay, what aboot an ornament?'

'Nar, they're cheap rubbish – made out o' chalk.'

'What aboot one o' them spinning ashtrays then?'

'Aye, that'll dee lass. Wrap that up youn 'en,' said Molly indicating to the assistant, 'An' then we can get out of this godforsaken place.'

The bingo caller didn't make eye contact, but was well aware of Molly's eyes burning into him as she went past him on the way out.

'You're quiet mother, are yer alright?' observed Kitty as they strolled down the promenade.

'Whey, aye lass. It's watter off a ducks back. Yer nar me Kitty, it'll tek more than a jumped up little shit like him to upset me. Ar'll tell yer what pet . . . How do yer fancy a nice bottle o' stout?'

'Sounds champion to me mother.'

A couple of minutes walk down the prom, they crossed over the road and went into the first pub they came to, The Ship – a place they'd frequented on previous trips to Whitley Bay.

'Hey up, it's Molly and Kitty!' came a voice from behind them as they stood at the bar.

'Ar divent need to look round to see who that is our Kitty. There's nee mistekking that gob – It's Mabel.'

Sure enough, sitting at a table amidst a number of empty glasses and stout bottles, were two good friends of theirs, Mabel and Betty.

'Ar might 'ave known ye two drunken buggers'd be in here. Do yer want another stout while we're ordering? That's if there's any left, the amount of empty bottles on your table.'

'Whey, we never turn a drink down Molly lass,' laughed Betty.

'An' there's plenty o' stout left,' stated Mabel. 'The landlord's only just brought up another crate from the cellar. We supped the first crate!'

Mabel and Betty had actually drank four bottles a piece, and were now nice and tiddly.

'Where've yer been tekking yer mother today Kitty?' inquired Mabel.

'Bingo of course, but that's a sore point at the moment,' she replied.

'Oh aye, why's that then?'

'Ar'll let me mother tell the tale. She's the one who gave 'em what for.'

Molly sat up straight and leaned forward. 'Whey, this young whipper snapper of a bingo caller was fiddling. He had this trollop sat playing an' winning every other game. It was so obvious he'd fixed it for her to win. Whey, ar couldn't contain meself any longer. Ar gave him a piece o' my mind. Yer nar me – ar divent stand on ceremony.'

'Yer do right Molly lass,' agreed Mabel. 'Ar'd 'ave done the same.'

'Aye, me too,' added Betty.

'What's this then? Is it a hen party, or just some old birds outing?'

'Yer cheeky bugger Tom Payne!' retorted Molly, good humouredly. 'We can quite easily tek our custom elsewhere yer nar.'

'Whey, ar wouldn't become bankrupt losing your custom that's for sure,' stated the landlord. 'Ye buggers only come in 'ere once a year.'

Tom was a single man and had been landlord at The Ship for nearly twenty years. He became acquainted with the 'Stanhope Clan' on their first day trip to Whitley Bay some fifteen years earlier. The leg pulling had become a regular annual event.

'Once a year's enough in this den of iniquity,' declared Mabel. 'An' these bottles o' stout are always covered in dust,' she complained.

'What do yer expect when they've been down the cellar fer the past year?' teased Tom.

'Yer mean to tell us we're supping old stout?' exclaimed Betty.

'You certainly are. Yer divent think ar would palm it off on me regular customers do yer?'

'Nar, but yer'd palm it off on us Tom Payne.'

'As if ar'd do a trick like that to you ladies. It's more than my life's worth.'

'Aye, yer've got that right bugger lugs,' agreed Molly.

'What time are yer ganning back home?' inquired Tom.

'Six o'clock,' replied Molly.

'Yer tekking a risk aren't yer?'

'How do yer mean like?' asked Kitty.

'Whey, the nights are drawing in rapidly now. If yer not back in yer coffins before nightfall – yer'll turn to dust.'

'There's only one vampire round here an' that's ye,' admonished Mabel. 'Yer could get blood out of a stone ye could.'

Tom sauntered off with the empty bottles and glasses, chuckling to himself. He enjoyed this annual banter, and he wished the

Stanhope Clan could be his regulars.

'Last orders please!'

'Whey, is it five to three already?' said Betty in surprise, looking at her watch. 'Shall we 'ave a short to finish with?'

They all agreed.

'Ar'll give you a hand,' volunteered Kitty as Betty made her way towards the bar, somewhat unsteadily.

'Four whiskies please Tom.'

'Coming right up madam.'

'Bah, ar can see why yer call 'em shorts,' complained Betty as Tom placed the drinks in front of her.

'Whey, it's a regular optic measure ar can assure you,' objected Tom.

'Arraway an' shite. Yer'll 'ave some way of interferring with 'em, yer crafty bugger – Or yer probably watter 'em down,' she slurred.

'Eeh . . . Betty lass, yer've a low opinion of me.'

'Well, yer canny blame me. The locals complain aboot yer wattering the beer down,' she said accusingly, winking at Kitty.

'Well, nee one's complained to me. Yer just a big stirrer Betty.'

'Ar could 'ave you fer slander. Defi . . . defam . . .'

'Defecation of character Betty?'

'Aye, that an' all.'

Tom chuckled to himself as he moved down the bar to serve another customer.

'Bottoms up!' they chorused, clinking their glasses together before downing the whisky in one go.

'That's better,' said Betty grimacing as the whisky hit her throat. 'So, what's on the agenda for this afternoon?' she gasped, looking at Molly and Kitty.

'Forty winks in a deckchair sounds attractive to me,' yawned Molly.

'Aye, that sounds alright to me an' all. What d'you say Mabel?'

'Champion, all this boozing 'as made me sleepy.'

'Ha way then, finish yer stout an' we'll get ganning,' ordered Molly.

'Hark at her! Who died an' made you queen?' remarked Betty,

good humouredly.

Knocking back the rest of their stout, they made for the exit, via the bar.

'Thank you landlord for your hospitality,' announced Molly.

'Thank God, ar thought you were never ganna leave,' joked Tom, before giving them all a peck on the cheek.

'Ar think we've supped enough rubbish fer one day,' declared Mabel.

'Arraway with yers. Ye buggers 'ad better 'urry up an' go afore I bar yer all,' he smiled affectionately.

'Cheerio Tom,' they chorused, making their way to the door. 'See yer next year!'

'Aye, God willing. Tek care ladies.'

Outside on the pavement, they had to get their bearings. The brightness of the sun was in complete contrast to the relative darkness inside the pub.

They crossed the road onto the promenade. Linking their arms together and giggling like teenagers, they started singing . . .

'Roll out the barrel
Let's have a barrel of fun
Roll out the barrel . . . '

'Whoops a daisy!' giggled Betty stumbling. Only the fact that they were linked together kept her upright. She laughed even more. 'Eeh . . . ar must be tiddlier than ar thought . . . Where's them deckchairs?'

'You're nothing more than an old lush, Betty Mills,' chuckled Mabel. 'We'd better sit you down, afore yer fall down.'

There wasn't a problem finding empty deckchairs at this time of day. They found a spot in the shade and sat themselves down.

'Ah . . . Just what the doctor ordered,' sighed Molly.

'You can say that again,' said Betty, drowsily closing her eyes.

Within minutes the 'Stanhope Clan' were in the land of nod.

Chapter 8

In the amusement park the lads and lasses were disembarking from the speedway ride. Having enjoyed it so much, they'd stayed on for a second ride.

'That was great,' enthused Sarah. 'Come on, let's go on again!'

This brought groans from the rest of the company, who declined.

'It gets a canny speed up like,' commented Billy. 'Ar thought ar was ganna fly off at one point.'

'Are you alright Alistair? Yer divent feel sick or owt, do yer?' mocked Roy with a silly smirk on his face.

'I'm fine Geordie. Compared with the rides we have back in Leeds when the fair comes, it's like going on a kids roundabout.'

'I'll second that,' agreed Karen. 'You tell him Alistair.'

'Hey, Roy!' shouted Billy, trying to make himself heard as the next record blasted out. 'Have yer got yer Brillo pad with yer? Yer hair's all ower the place!'

'Very funny ginger nut.'

'It's three o'clock,' commented Karen. 'Anyone fancy a coke?'

The girls all agreed.

'What about you lot?' Sarah asked the lads.

'I nar a good cafe,' announced Roy. 'We gan there every year. They call it Marco's – it's not far from here. The owner's a pal of mine. If he nars yer with me, yer'll get a discount.'

The girls looked at each other in mock disbelief.

'He never stops does he?' said Katy derisively.

'He's a blooming pain in the backside,' added Laura.

At least Roy was right for once in saying that Marco's was nearby. The Italian cafe was barely two minutes walk away, on the sea front.

'Marco!' proclaimed Roy, making his way towards the counter, the others close behind. 'How yer ganning, my little Italian meatball? One cuppa el coffeo Marco.'

'I'm a Italiano, notta de Spanish, el boyo – you daft a prat o. Who a de 'ell a are you anyways? I notta know any a Spanish – el Geordios. What about a you Karl?'

'No boss, I notta know neither,' shrugged Marco's assistant.

'Divent ye start an' all Karl,' warned Roy. 'Ha way Marco, stop messing me aboot. Ar's deeing o' thirst here man.'

'Okey, dokey . . . How are a you Roy? Is it a year a gonna by all a ready? It a notta feel like a month since a you were a spouting a the bigga mouth off in here.'

'Hey, less of the cheek Mr Whippy. Give us an espresso, or whatever you call it, an' less of yer lip.'

'Cappuccino . . . Uno cuppa da frothy coffee coming a right up. What a 'appen to your head? You gotta the Indians in Stanhope?'

'Whey, ar divent nar what yer wittering on aboot, my little gondola friend.'

'I thought a you must 'ave a the Indians, with you a being scalped.'

'We are the wag today aren't we? Did yer swallow a crap joke book fer breakfast lardy? Ye an' Karl should get together wi' Stuart an' form a trio. Yer could call yer sens the Three Grease Balls.'

'Ah . . . You're just a jealous. Is it a true they call a you de porcu-a-pine a Roy back in a the Stanhope?'

'Just hurry up with that coffee Marconi, an' none of yer mucky cups wi' lipstick all ower.'

'And how are a de rest of you lads? Keeping a well I hope?'

Billy spoke up, 'Aye, champion, canna complain like Marco.'

'You a surprise a me – Still a going round a with a de knob head.'

'We canna get rid of him man,' sighed Billy. 'He sticks to us like shit to a blanket.'

'I see you gotta the pretty ladies with you today. Where a you a come from girls? Notta the Stanhope I hope – land of a the hillbillies.'

'No, we're on a day trip from Leeds,' announced Laura. 'You've heard of Leeds United haven't you? The best football team in the world . . . Right girls?'

'Yeah!' they all cheered.

'I am a the sorry ladies. I can notta agree with you there. Leeds a United – they a bag a the sheet a. Excuse a my French ladies, but we have a the best a football teams in Italy. Inter Milan, Juventus, Lazio . . . Ar've a no need to go on.'

'If they're that good, then what are yer doing ower here like?' sneered Roy.

'I'm a here to run a the business and a culture you English. Also, I teach a you how to play a the football.'

Roy thought he himself was good at talking, but he'd met his match in Marco. He was certainly his equal in the verbal diarrhoea department. 'Whey, how do you teach football? Even if yer were capable of it, yer've still got a cafe to run.'

'I train a the players on a Tuesday and a Thursday nights.'

'Oh aye, an' which team do yer coach then, Newcastle? Sunderland? . . . Or mebbe it's Middlesborough?'

'No, I coach a none a them teams. I teach a the Whitley Bay United. They a good team.'

'You can take on our Ken, she's a good footballer,' proclaimed Laura.

'Stop calling me Ken,' objected Katy. 'Anyway, I don't play much soccer now that I'm older.'

'So, you are what a they call a the tommy boy, yes?'

'It's tomboy – And no, I'm not one. I used to be . . . but not any more.'

'Arr . . . I see a.'

'Whitley Bay?' mocked Roy. 'You canna be very ambitious. Yer haven't set yer sights very high, that's fer sure. Stanhope Working Mens Club could beat that bunch of amateurs – an' they're shite.'

'Now you take a the peez, Spikey. Since I start a the training two month back, we notta lose a the one single match.'

'Whey, yer won't 'ave lost a game Pepe – They've not played fer nine weeks – it's the summer break man.'

'That a beside a the point . . . We still notta lose a game.'

'Oh, I give up. Ar's off fer a sit down,' grumbled Roy. 'It's like talking to a brick wall.'

'What a can I get a you lovely young ladies? These a boys can wait. Ladies should always a be first. That a Roy . . . He's an ig-a-noramous – no gotta any the manners.'

'What was that yer said Marconi?' piped up Roy. 'Ar hope yer not talking aboot me bonny lad!'

'Keep a your 'air on – what a little you 'ave. I talk a to the ladies.'

'Watch him girls! He'll be tekking yer in the back to show yer 'is bolognese – the dirty old bugger!'

'Keep a the nose out a you big ears.'

To which Roy gave Marco the V sign after he'd turned his back on him.

'Do you want coke or coffee our young 'en?' Laura asked Katy.

'I'll 'ave a Coca-Cola,' replied Katy.

'Do you want a bag o' crisps or owt?'

'Get us a Kit-Kat Loz.'

'Right, two cokes and two Kit-Kats please Mr Marco.'

'Karl! Get a the two Coca-Colas and a two Keet-Kats!'

'Coming a right up boss!'

Karen and Sarah took their order and went and sat with Laura and Katy on the table next to Roy.

Alistair settled for a Coca-Cola and a bag of crisps, while Billy and Stuart ordered beefburgers before sitting down.

'Divent get yer heed too near that grill Marco Polo,' goaded Roy. 'If that half inch of Brylcreem catches fire, we'll all gan up in smoke!'

'Shut up a yer face – hedgehog head. You come in a my cafe once a year and cause a more havoc than a my regular customers do all a the year round.'

'Ar think yer'd miss me . . . It's the highlight of your year. Go on Pepe . . . admit it,' taunted Roy, handing round his cigarettes, safe in the knowledge that only Billy would accept one – the rest of them being non smokers.

Karl strolled over to the boys table and placed two beefburgers in front of Stuart and Billy.

'Bloody hell!' exclaimed Roy. 'Ar's glad ar didn't order one o' them shrivelled up things. Ar've seen bigger meatballs!'

Karl shook his head. 'You'd a never be 'appy. Every year a you come in a the cafe . . . It's a complain, complain. I think a you love to extract a the urine.'

'What's with the big words? Why divent yer just come out an' say it – I tek the piss! No need to be long winded Boris.'

'I no understand. What is this a Boris you call a me? My name is a Karl.'

'Whey, 'ave yer not heard of the actor Boris Karlos? Yer nar . . . Karlos – Karl?' stated Roy cockily.

'How a you say? Ar divent nar what a you on aboot,' said Karl, doing his best to imitate Roy before putting the icing on the cake by adding, 'But I have heard of a the Boris Karloff . . . '

'Forget it,' said an irritated Roy. 'Gan an' clean the toilets or summat – mek yer sen useful.'

'Ar've got a no lavatory brush. If you come a with me, I could stick a your big head down a the sheet pot.'

The lads and lasses laughed heartily, thoroughly enjoying Roy's demise.

'Very funny Karlos. Yer winna be so cocky when ar report yer to the immigration board fer being an illegal immigrant. Ar nar all aboot ye wops, stowing away on them pasta boats. Coming ower here an' oppening up barber shops without any training. A load o' poofters man – rubbing yer balls up against yer customers. Ar's not daft – I've got you lot weighed up. Yer flatten everyone's heed down wi' gallons o' Brylcreem, so they canna see the bollocks yer've made o' cutting their hair.'

'Rubeesh! How a you say? You talk a through the ass.'

'It's all true man. Hey Karl . . . Do you play for Whitley Bay United?'

'No, I notta play a the football. It a too energetic a game for me.'

'That's strange. Ar thought all ye Italians were natural athletes like.'

'What a make a you think that for?'

'Whey, during the war, when we British were after yer, yer dropped yer weapons an' ran like hell. They said they couldn't see yer fer dust. It's not fer me to say like – an' ar's only quoting here . . . but word 'as it that you were cowards.'

'Absolute a the crap! That was just a the propaganda. Italian soldiers? They a the best in the world.'

'Aye, they are, at ganning backwards,' scorned Roy.

'You talk a the complete sheet.'

'Karl, come and talk to us,' said Karen. 'You'll get more sense out of us.'

'Watch it wi' them lasses Karl,' smirked Roy. 'They're only after yer salami.'

'Is a everything to your a satisfaction young a ladies?' asked Karl smiling at the girls.

'Yes, it's fine thank you,' replied Laura.

'I notta see you in a here before. Is it a your first a time you come to Whitley bay?'

'Yeah, we usually go to Blackpool,' said Katy. 'There's loads to do there, even if it's raining. The Pleasure Beach is brilliant.'

'Yeah, you're in you're element there aren't you Ken? Hundreds of slot machines to go at,' commented Sarah sarcastically.

'I've grown out of that phase,' declared Katy. 'Well, nearly . . . I don't go on them quite as often – an' stop calling me Ken.'

'He's quite dishy,' Karen whispered to Sarah. 'I wouldn't mind taking him back home with me.'

'Well, I'll be right behind you in the queue for him,' giggled Sarah.

'You'll have to excuse these two Karl, they're man eaters,' warned Laura.

'Why they eat a the men? Is it notta illegal to eat a the people in England? Ar thought only the cannibals eat a the people,' joked Karl.

The girls laughed, warming to Karl and his sense of humour.

Laura noticed how Stuart kept looking over towards her, trying to act casual, but without much success. Every time Laura made eye contact, he shyly averted his gaze.

'Is Marco your father Karl?' asked Katy.

'No, he notta my father, he is a my uncle. I work a four years for him. He is a how you say? Okay most a the time.'

'How old are you Karl?'

'Ah, that a would be telling.'

'Well, yeah, course it would, that's why I asked you,' said Katy sarcastically.

'You're a cheeky a young lady. What a the age you think is me?'

'Well now . . . ' she thought. 'I'd say about twenty.'

'And what a you think Kareen?'

'Mmm . . . let's see . . . About twenty four I'd say.'

'Your a turn to guess Sarah.'

'I'll go fer about twenty two-ish.'

'And last but notta the least . . . Laura.'

'I'm no good at peoples ages. Go on, I'll say nineteen, just off the top of me head,' she said, not really interested, having noticed Stuart looking at her only to look away again as she made eye contact with him.

'Sarah guess a my right age. I'se a twenty two.'

'Hooray!' said Sarah, clapping her hands. 'Do I get a prize? A free bottle o' coke or summat?'

'No, I'm afraid a not. Marco . . . how you say? Tight as ducks arse. He a flip his lid if he see me take a the bottle without a paying.'

'I'll 'ave a kiss then, or will Marco flip his lid over that an' all?'

'Okey, dokey, I give a the kiss – but just on a the cheek.'

'Ooh, I'll settle for that . . . Go on then,' said Sarah, saucily offering Karl her cheek.

He gave her a peck and blushed, instantly creating raucous cheers from the lads and lasses.

'Hey up, yer wanna watch that Boris girls,' proclaimed Roy. 'Next year he **will** be slapping his salami on the table!'

'Trust you,' scorned Karen. 'You've got a dirty mind.'

Roy laughed. It was water off a ducks back, as usual.

'Have you got a girlfriend Karl?' asked Laura.

'Well, I 'ave a the girlfriend, but me notta in a the serious reshipalation.'

'Relationship you mean,' laughed Laura.

'Yes . . . That a the word.'

'Don't a you listen to the lying little sheet!' shouted Marco from behind the counter. 'He's a been engaged for a two a the years! He's a getting a married at Chreestmas!'

Marco was lying through his teeth because he didn't want to be left out of this light hearted bullshit. His mundane existence, working in the cafe day after day was monotonous, and any good humoured banter was a welcome distraction from the daily grind.

'Karl! How could you tell us all them lies?' tutted Laura disapprovingly.

'An' we were just getting to like you,' added Sarah.

'I no lie. That Marco – He notta tell a you the truth. He – a how you say? Pull a the leg . . . mix with a the big spoon.'

'So you're not engaged then?' asked Karen.

'Definately not. Look at Marco . . . He a laughing his a daft head off.'

'Marco, stop mixing it!' called Sarah.

Marco was noisily frothing a cappuccino, a huge grin on his face. 'Hey, I only have a the joke, but you still notta wanna believe what a Karl tell you – he a big a dreamer.'

'Ah . . . Leesten to him,' said Karl with contempt. 'You gotta no room to talk. At least I'm notta the married . . . I say the no more.'

Karl's statement must have hit a sour note. Marco's silence spoke volumes. Although Karl knew all about Marco's private life, he wouldn't divulge it to all and sundry.

'Is he two timing his wife then, your uncle?' quizzed Katy.

'You are a very nosey a young lady. Marco – he a very happily married man with two leetle bambinos. He a faithful to his wife,' he lied.

Marco had been having an affair with a young girl who worked for him sometimes at the weekend. Together, they spent a lot of time in the storeroom. Marco had feared on occasions that Karl would let the cat out of the bag and expose his 'bit on the side' –

but he was just mischief making, and if the push came to the shove, Karl would be the soul of discretion.

Roy shuffled past Karl making his way to the toilet.

'Hey, hedge-a-hog head! called Marco. 'Make a sure you notta smoke any a that funny tobacco in a my toilet. How you call? . . . Marijuanny.'

'Marijuana, you idiot – An' ar've never touched the stuff,' declared Roy truthfully. 'Ar's quite happy with me Cadets. Ar's not one o' them scruffy beatnik types yer get in here yer nar.'

'You could a fooled a me.'

'Bloody cheek,' mumbled Roy opening the door of the gents. After relieving himself, he sat down on the toilet seat and lit a cigarette. Drawing deeply on it, he exhaled the smoke with a contented sigh. 'Just what the doctor ordered . . . '

'Karl!'

'Yes boss.'

'Are a you on a the strike? There'a a customers want a serving here. Leave a them a young ladies alone an' come and get a some work done, or I dock a your wages.'

'I'm a coming right away boss – just a wiping the tables down. Cheerio ladies. It a nice a talking with you.'

'Bye Karl,' they chorused, disappointed that he was leaving them.

Roy strutted arrogantly out of the toilet, his mouth immediately back in motion. 'Bah, yer wanna get that shit 'ouse cleaned! The floor's covered in piss. Even the bluebottles are wearing welly boots!'

'It's a notta the peez,' objected Karl. 'I swill a the floor with water and a the bleach, you cheeky booger.'

'Whey, what was in that coffee I 'ad, a laxative? 'Cause it went straight through me. Ar farted an' pebble dashed yer walls. Somebody's left a great big logger in there an' all. Yer canna tell me yer clean them bogs regular, because it must 'ave been there ages – it's covered in green mould. Kilroy probably left it in 1960 because he's signed fer it on yer wall.'

'Marco put his finger to his lips, 'Shush . . . Stop talking about a the sheet pot. You put a the customers off a their food.'

'Sorry Marco,' apologised Roy in a whisper. 'Ar didn't think.'

'Well, that a the trouble with you. Opening the big a mouth before engaging a the brain.' Marco shook his head and carried on wiping down the counter.

'Turn round a minute man,' said Billy to Roy as he rejoined them.

'What's up like?' puzzled Roy.

'Whey, there's summat all ower yer back. It looks like whitewash.' Billy proceeded to brush down Roy's back and shoulders with his hand. 'It's coming off nee problem,' he assured him.

'Ar've a good mind to claim damages off Marconi. Ruddy whitewash on an inside toilet . . . Yer'd think the little Italian miser was destitute – tight sod. Ar mean, what would it cost fer a tin of emulsion? Bugger all, that's what.'

'That's it bonny lad,' announced Billy, finishing off Roy's brushing down with a slap on the back. 'Ar've got it all off.'

'Cheers my little carrot headed friend. I'll remember yer in me will – don't let me ferget,' he said ruffling Billy's hair. 'Right, is everybody ready fer the off?'

'Aye,' agreed the lads, getting up from the table.

'Are you ready girls?' asked Stuart, purposely hanging back so he could walk with Laura.

'Yeah, I suppose so,' replied Karen. 'Ha way girls, are you all ready? Hang on a minute,' she said as they made ready to leave, 'I'm just going for summat to take out.'

'What are you getting?' asked Laura.

'Karl . . .' replied Karen mischievously.

'You wish . . . Come on man eater, let's get off.'

They all said their farewells to Marco and Karl – Karen somewhat reluctantly – and made for the exit. Stuart managed to squeeze himself between the girls next to Laura. Roy, bringing up the rear, was determined to get in one last dig before leaving their hosts to return to some semblance of normality.

'Whey, ar'd like to say it's been a pleasure my little Italian lard heeds. Ar'd like to . . . but ar'd be lying. Old Turner's pig sty's cleaner than this cess pit. Some decent coffee wouldn't 'ave gone amiss neither. Ar nar what cheap shite yer buy from that cash an' carry. Yer buy them 'alf a crown two gallon catering tins. Jo Jo's cafe in Stanhope – they use that crap. Yer all the same man . . . a bunch o' racketeers the lot of yers.'

'You – how a you say? Ah, yes – talk a the load a the bollocks,' retorted Marco. 'There's a nothing wrong with a my coffee. It a come direct a from my native country, Italy. Finest coffee in a da world. Notta the cheap a neither . . . very expensive. In a fact, I sell it at too a lower the price to my customers. Still . . . that a me all over – generous a to a the fault. What a I do? It just a my nature. I get a the embarrassed because a my customers – they call a me the kind, big a hearted Marco. Sometimes, I blush a leetle you know, me being the modest man.'

'Bah, yer've missed yer calling Marconi. Ye shouldn't be working in a poxy cafe, selling curled up sandwiches and inferior coffee. Nar . . . Italian politics are more in your line. Ar could picture it now – Marco – the overseas minister of bullshit.'

'You think a you're a the funny hedge-a-hog head,' said Marco, ushering Roy through the door. 'Me think it time for a you to go, before I give a you the thick ear.'

Roy puffed his chest out, 'Oh aye, ye an' whose army? Divent think ar's scared of you – or Boris there. Ar feel ar must warn the pair of yers that I'm the Weardale karate champion three years running. It'll tek more than a couple of Italian greaseballs to see the back of me.'

'Karl . . . !'

'Yes boss?'

'Put a the big mouth outside a my cafe please,' ordered Marco.

'No problem boss,' said Karl, coming out from behind the counter.

'Right! Ar canna stand aboot all day talking to the likes o' ye two,' waffled Roy, hastily making his exit. 'My colleagues will be fretting without their leader. I'll see yer later – That's if the health inspectors divent shut yer down first!' Satisfied he'd got the last word in, Roy swiftly closed the door behind him.

Marco looked across at Karl, 'They broke a the mould a with that one,' he chuckled.

Chapter 9

'What yer been deeing in there all that time?' grumbled Billy. 'We've been waiting that long for yer we've got a suntan.'

'Stop exaggerating man,' admonished Roy. 'The Brylcreem boys wanted my advice on how to maximise their profit margin.'

'Oh no,' groaned Alistair, 'Here we go again – more bull. What did yer tell 'em then? That they should start selling pease pudding?'

'No, clever clogs. If yer must nar, I telt 'em to get some decent up to date records put on that antique jukebox o' theirs, an' to tek off that Mario Lanza shite. Secondly, come evening, when they've got rid of all the old fogeys – to let the young 'ens in through the back door. Yer nar, like Bert an' Betty dee wi' Jo Jo's. They'll mek plenty of extra brass that way.'

'Ah, but Jo Jo's is different,' Alistair pointed out. 'Bert and Betty aren't exactly rolling in money opening up a few late nights for us. They only do it for the social side of it, not fer profit.'

'Typical negative Yorkshireman. What ar mean is . . . Jo Jo's is in Stanhope man. Yer nar, a village . . . ? Whey Marco's on the other hand is in Whitley Bay.'

'Bloody hell, it's Sherlock Holmes!' mocked Alistair.

'Shut up an' listen a minute! Ar think yer'll find Whitley Bay is more populated than Stanhope. If Marco pulls his finger out, his poxy cafe could be packed with punters every night o' the week. Ar hope he does well.'

'Hey up, he's got his Jekyll an' Hyde head on again,' derided Alistair.

'No bonny lad. Ar hope he does well 'cause ar's on twenty percent of the extra profits made through my business skills.'

'Arraway an' shite,' rebuked Billy. 'Do we look as if we've just fallen off a Christmas tree?'

'Whey, yer give me the needle,' chortled Roy, to which no one else laughed.

'Anyone any ideas on what to do now?' asked Karen.

'Let's go on the beach,' suggested Katy. 'We can 'ave a paddle in the sea.'

They all agreed.

'Tell yer what lads – How aboot us all chipping in an' buying a football?' suggested Billy. 'We can 'ave a kick aboot then.' Again, they all agreed. 'Great stuff – Ha way, there's a Woollies just up the road.'

Reaching Woolworths, they all trooped in. The boys immediately went in search of a football.

'Hoy, Alistair!' bellowed Roy, purposely making sure that everyone in the shop could hear him.

'What do you want?' growled Alistair angrily, not very happy at the volume of Roy's mouth.

'There's some buckets an' spades here our kid! They're half price in the sale!'

'Then buy yer sen a set!' retorted Alistair. 'It'll give yer summat to do on the beach, because yer crap at football!'

Roy knew this to be true, but wouldn't admit it, especially in front of the Yorkshire lasses. He'd bluff his way out of it somehow, when it came to the actual kick about.

After purchasing a football, they left Woolworths and crossed the main road onto the promenade.

Stuart took hold of Laura's hand as they crossed the road, only to quickly let go of it on the other side, still unsure of himself.

It was relatively quiet on this stretch of beach compared with the central area, nearer the town centre.

Billy kicked the ball high and long. It went beyond the soft dry sand, landing on the damp firmer area nearer the sea where the tide had gone out, scattering several seagulls in it's wake.

All the lads raced like fury to be the first to reach the newly purchased ball.

'Just look at 'em,' laughed Laura. 'They're like little kids.'

'Do you think Stuart'll be alright on his own?' asked Katy mischievously.

'He's not on his own,' stated Laura. 'What are you on about little sister?'

'I mean, without somebody to hold his hand.'

'That's very funny our Ken. All he did was see me across the road, there's nowt wrong in that is there?'

'Give over, you're like a pair of lovebirds,' accused Karen grinning like a cheshire cat.

'There's nothing in it,' protested Laura sitting down on the steps and removing her shoes. 'We just get on together.'

The girls said no more, but ran off giggling across the soft warm sand.

'Let's play attack and defence,' suggested Billy.

'Great, ar'll gan in goal!' volunteered Roy, safe in the knowledge that his lack of footballing skills would be less obvious as goalkeeper.

'Right then, me an' Stuart against ye two,' organised Billy. 'We'll attack first.'

'Aye okay. Ar'll mark the goal area out,' said Roy. 'Alistair! Lend us yer cloth cap fer one of the goal posts!'

'It's a good job you're in goal Roy, 'cause there's no way Stuart an' Billy are gonna get the ball past that big fat head of yours,' mocked Alistair.

'Whey, let's face it Yorky – Ye'd be no good in goal would yer? Yer like a stick insect. If the ball hit yer, yer'd snap in two!'

Roy looked around for two good sized stones to use as goal posts. He put one down on the sand and then took six paces to obtain the approximate width of the goal. There he placed the second stone. Picking up a razor shell, he marked out the attacking area. Any shots at goal had to be from outside the designated area of sand. Any scored inside the box would be instantly disqualified. Of course, arguments always ensued on the validity of the goals being this or that side of the line.

It didn't take long for Billy and Stuart to score three goals, the required number before the attackers took their turn in defence. Roy diving about like a theatrical clown didn't help. They might just as well have been playing without a football. The only time he touched the ball was after a goal was scored when he had to tramp across the beach and retrieve it. Even then, he objected at the unfairness of being nothing more than a glorified ball boy, proclaiming that Alistair should fetch the ball, him being the youngest.

Alistair counteracted this remark by reminding Roy that if he actually saved the ball, his long trek wouldn't be neccessary.

The girls, having finished their romp through the sand, had sat down and were now watching the boys at play.

Roy had noticed them, and his heart sank. With the girls watching, the cat would be out of the bag. The shortcomings in his inability to play football, would now be revealed for all to see.

'Come on Alistair, show 'em 'ow it's done!' encouraged Sarah.

'Come on Stuart, get 'em tackled!' shouted Laura excitedly.

The ball broke loose, landing at Roy's feet but Stuart blocked Roy's view of goal. Instead of passing the ball square, where Alistair stood in acres of space – he went for glory. Needless to say, his shot went well wide of the goal post.

'Whoo . . . Hard lines Roy! Another ten feet to the right an' that would've been a goal,' mocked Alistair scornfully, shaking his head in disbelief. 'I was clear Roy! Why didn't yer pass it square to me? I was clear through!'

'Ah . . . get knotted. You'd 'ave missed anyway. I only shot wide 'cause a crab nipped me foot just as ar went to hit the ball.'

Embarrassment didn't exist in Roy's world. He'd surely make a great politician some day. He'd be in his element . . . Standing there . . . spewing out lie after lie, without batting an eyelid. He'd definately have found his forte.

'Hey, Roy!' shouted Katy. 'The idea is to kick the ball between them big pebbles there – not kick it into the sea!'

'Whey, ar canny help it if a crustacean decided to nip me just as ar were aboot to score!' protested Roy.

'What's a crustacean when it's at home?' shouted Katy.

'Eeh . . . are yer all thick from Yorkshire? A crustacean is a hard shelled animal. In my case, it was a crab. Yer nar . . . that thing with the claws? That's what pinched me foot. Ask our Alistair, he's an expert on crabs – His nuts are covered in 'em!'

'Bollocks!' objected Alistair.

'Same thing . . . !'

'If you concentrated on the football instead of your mouth, we might get somewhere.'

'Ooh . . . we are touchy my little Yorky. It's only a game man, not life an' death. Stop being so **crabby**.'

Billy kicked the ball, a little over enthusiastically, back into the field of play.

'I'll get it!' shouted Alistair, running after the ball, knowing there was no chance of Roy exerting himself and going after it. After retrieving the ball, Alistair set off back to the others playing 'keepy uppy' on the way. (Keeping control of the ball in the air and not letting it touch the ground).

'Alright clever dick, the girls 'ave seen yer showing off. Just get on with the game,' said Roy, scathingly.

As Alistair approached nearer to goal, Stuart advanced out to tackle him. Against Alistair's better judgement, he passed the ball to Roy, who was no more than a couple of yards from goal.

Roy thought that with only Billy in goal, this was his big chance for glory. Mindful of the girls watching, he swung his right leg back to shoot. Unfortunately, when bringing his foot down, it stubbed into the sand, just inches away from the ball. Roy fell, arse over tit, face down in the sand.

'Everyone laughed uncontrollably. This was certainly the highlight of the day so far, suffice to say, except for poor Roy, who was lying prostrate on the beach.

'What happened this time Roy? Did yer trip ower a lobster, or was it an octopus grabbed yer wi' one of it's tentacles?' laughed Billy, thoroughly enjoying Roy's misfortune.

Roy leapt to his feet, brushing himself down. Then, feigning injury, he hobbled along. 'What yer laughing for? Ar've sprained me ankle, that's why ar missed the ball. Ar would've scored.'

'Orh . . . Poor Roy. We believe you,' lied Karen trying to sound sympathetic.

Roy hopped over towards the girls. Sitting down beside them, he groaned in mock pain. 'Sorry lads, ar canna play on. My injury is too severe.'

'Oh no!' cried Alistair dramatically. 'Alas! How will I manage without my star player?'

'Our Ken'll tek his place, won't yer Ken?' volunteered Laura on Katy's behalf.

'I suppose so,' replied Katy trying to sound nonchalant, while secretly dying to show off her footballing skills. 'And don't call me Ken.'

Alistair passed to Katy on the right wing. She set off towards goal, a determined look on her face.

Stuart blocked her way, resolute not to let a girl get the better of him. Katy nutmegged him, (kicking the ball between his legs) the ball landing at Alistair's feet. Standing in a centre forward position, hardly believing his luck, Alistair just side footed the ball past Billy's outstretched legs for a goal.

'Good pass Ken – I mean Katy,' complimented Alistair, quickly correcting himself.

'Yer supposed to tackle 'em, not open yer legs to be nutmegged,' said Billy reprovingly to Stuart.

'Whey, if you're so good, you defend an' ar'll tek ower in goal.'

'Right, yer on lard heed.'

The two boys swopped places. Stuart kicked the ball high and long across the beach.

'I'll get it!' shouted Katy running after the ball like a champion racehorse.

'Go on Kenny, you show 'em 'ow it's done!' shouted Sarah after her.

'The name's Katy!' she reminded Sarah with a withering look.

On reaching the ball, Katy turned and sped full steam ahead towards goal.

Billy steeled himself ready for the onslaught, determined not to let her past him. He shuffled his feet, swaying from side to side. 'Yer winna nutmeg me like yer did Billy Fury!' he declared confidently.

'Okay, carrot top,' said Katy obligingly flicking the ball swiftly over his head like greased lightening and swerving her body round him before swiftly back heeling the ball to Alistair. Alistair greatfully accepted the ball and tapped it past Stuart into the corner of the goal.

'Easy, easy . . . ' chanted the girls.

Billy turned on Stuart. 'Why didn't yer dive an' save it! 'Ave yer got lead in yer winkle pickers or are yer scared of ruffling yer 'air up? 'Cause ar wouldn't worry on that front boyo . . . It'd tek a stick o' dynamite to separate that Brylcreem from yer cranium.'

'Whey, ye've no room to talk,' derided Stuart. 'Ken – ar mean Katy, went through yer like a dose of Andrews liver salts.'

'Only 'cause ar had sand in me eye man. Ar was just ganna dispossess her of the ball, when a gust of wind blew some sand in me face.'

'Arraway an' shite. It's because yer crap, carrot top.'

'Piss off greaser,' retorted Billy angrily, as they squared up to one another.

'Who's for a paddle in the sea?' announced Karen diplomatically as she and Laura stepped between the boys.

'Good idea,' agreed Laura. 'We can all cool off a bit,' she added linking her arm through Stuart's and heading for the sea.

The rest of the group followed chattering away, any friction already evaporated.

'Roy!' exclaimed Sarah.

'What's up?'

'Where's yer limp gone? Yer walking normal. What 'appened to yer sprained ankle?'

'Oh . . . that? Whey, ar's so super fit, ar heal in no time. They divent call me the iron man of Weardale fer nowt yer nar.'

'The Weardale con man more like,' muttered Alistair. 'You feigned injury to cover up your lack of football skills, admit it. Not that I'm complaining mind. When Katy took your place, it was all over, bar the shouting. We never looked back. She's more talent in her little toe than you have in yer whole body.'

'Steady on Yorky, just because yer won. Yeah, fair enough, Katy wasn't bad, but ye've nowt to crow aboot. You were shite.'

'Sour grapes Roy. Yer a bad loser.'

'Whey, if yer must nar, ar'll admit it – football bores me. That's why ar divent try ower much.'

'Yer'll tell us owt,' smirked Alistair.

Leaving their footwear at a safe distance from the sea, the lads with their pants rolled up to their knees charged straight in, whooping, shouting and kicking. They ventured further into deeper, cooler water which was welcome after their kick about on such a hot day. It wasn't long before their jeans and trousers were soaked through. They didn't care that the water was now well above knee level.

Of course, it wasn't for the girls to go dashing headlong straight into the sea. They tentatively put their toes in first, retreating and squealing, venturing a little further each time, until they were confident enough to stay put in six inches of water.

The lads plotted mischievously, then, they gradually closed the distance between themselves and the girls. At a signal from Billy, they all charged past the girls, flat footed, to cause maximum sea spray, hence soaking the girls thoroughly.

The girls ran screaming from the shallow waters, cursing the boys en route. Stuart chased after them. Catching up, he swept a screaming Laura off her feet and carried her back into the sea, threatening to take her out further.

'Put me down!' she yelled. 'If you drop me Stuart, you're dead! I mean it!'

'Orh . . . Is the big baby scared o' the watter?' he teased.

The waves were now reaching above his knees. 'Shall ar drop her in!' he shouted, turning to the rest of the group.

'Yeah . . . Go on!' they all jeered, encouraging him to go ahead and do it.

'You do, an' I swear, I'll never speak to you again Stuart,' threatened Laura.

Stuart had no intentions of upsetting Laura, so decided his little jape should end before he caused any damage to their blossoming relationship. 'Ha way then, bonny lass. Ar'll let yer off this time,' he reassured her, making his way back to the shore with aching arms.

'A wise move Stewpot. You've just escaped with your life,' she proclaimed.

There was the expected jeers from the rest of the group, 'Yer coward, yer big chicken, scaredy cat.' The barrage of derisory remarks went right over Stuarts head.

Roy was dumbstruck for once. He couldn't believe that this self confident person carrying a girl from the sea, was the same life long, timid friend of his.

After Stuart gently placed Laura back down on the terra firma, they all retrieved their belongings and headed back towards the promenade.

Roy bent down and put his hand in one of the pools of water in the sand. 'Hey, Alistair . . . '

'Yeah?'

'Here yer are, a mussel for yer – seeing as yer've not got any,' he chortled.

'Hey, I've got a good idea,' said Alistair. 'Why not stick it in your big mouth an' chew on it for the rest of the day. Give us all a break from the verbal diarrhoea you constantly talk.'

'You tell 'im Alistair lad,' congratulated Karen, patting Alistair on the back.

'What the heck's verbal diarrhoea?' asked Katy.

'Basically, it means he talks a load of shit,' explained Sarah. 'Yer should've said that in the first place Alistair.'

'I didn't want to appear uncouth in front of you ladies. I'm not like Roy.'

'Creep . . . ' sneered Roy. 'Why divent yer tek 'im back to Leeds with yers? The skinny Yorkshire puff.'

'Well thank God he's not like you,' rebuked Karen. 'We've got some spare seats on our coach, most folks 'ave gone to Blackpool. You can come back to Leeds with us Alistair, if you want. Take no notice of yer arrogant cousin.'

Alistair stuck out his chest, putting on a front. 'He doesn't bother me. It's in one ear an' straight out the other. I'm used to him,' he insisted, shrugging his shoulders.

'Ar've just proved my point,' boasted Roy. 'Yer see girls . . . All this taunting of our Alistair is fer his own good. Ar've brought him out of his shell.'

Roy was building fences now, trying to come across as some sort of learned saviour in paving the right path for Alistair to follow. The bullshit ineviatably flowed forth. 'Not so long ago, he wouldn't say 'boo' to a goose. Ar mean for instance, just then . . . he answered back, full of confidence. That's the result of my teaching – my great leadership. Brain surgeons'll pay a fortune fer my heed when ar's deed.'

It didn't wash with the girls.

'Come on, you're just a bully and a big mouth,' said Karen accusingly.

'Give ower. Ar's what yer call a character with personality. Some would say . . . a national treasure.'

'Urgh, pass me the sick bucket,' said Sarah, sticking two fingers in her mouth.

'Give ower. Yer love me really . . . All the girls dee, don't deny it.'

After derogatory groans, the group decided not to encourage Roy's self appraisal any longer – Best to leave him to himself in his own little fantasy world.

'Have yer seen them two behind us?' whispered Karen, nudging Sarah. 'The lovebirds, Romeo an' Juliet?'

Sarah and Katy looked round to see Laura and Stuart some distance behind, hand in hand chattering away, oblivious to any one around them.

Reaching the promenade, they sat down on an empty bench to brush the sand off their feet and to put their shoes and socks back on.

'Whey, there's no need to put them back on,' sneered Roy, referring to Stuarts socks. 'They'll walk back home on their own Stewpot.'

'How d'yer mean? yer cheeky sod,' objected Stuart. 'Granted, they're a bit stiff – What d'yer expect in this weather? Ar was running aboot delivering milk in 'em this morning – but they were clean on. Ar put on a fresh pair every day.'

'Aye, an' yer get bathed once a year, whether you need one or not. Ar bet ye think he's got B O divent yer Laura?'

'Get away, he smells lovely . . . An' there's nowt wrong with his socks,' she insisted, picking one up and sniffing it to prove her point. 'On second thoughts though . . . '

'Divent ye start,' laughed Stuart, embarrassed at Laura smelling one of his socks.

'Urgh! How can you our Loz?' exclaimed Katy.

'What's up with you little sister? They divent – I mean, they don't smell.'

'Ooh . . . It must be love,' teased Sarah.

'I'm off to the toilet,' announced Katy, spotting a public convenience over the road. 'Anyone coming?'

Karen and Sarah got to their feet, ready to follow Katy.

'Laura!' bawled Karen. 'Do yer think yer can pull yerself away from Stuart long enough for a pee?'

'Yeah, alright – Keep yer 'air on, I'm coming,' chuntered Laura, getting up reluctantly and following the girls.

'We'll meet you outside the bog!' shouted Stuart.

'Okay!' replied Laura, smiling and giving him a little wave as she disappeared into the toilet.

'Ar's off to the gents, ar divent nar aboot ye lot,' said Roy, throwing the football in the direction of Alistair who deftly caught it. 'Ye can carry it fer a while. Ha way, let's gan ower the road.'

'Yes sir, owt else sir? Yer don't want me to polish yer scabby winkle pickers or perhaps shine your head, do you sir?' said Alistair sarcastically.

'No, just carry the football sonny an' stop yer chelping.'

Roy and Stuart disappeared into the gents, while Alistair and Billy went inside an amusement arcade just a a few yards away. They decided to sample the machines on display, and went to the money changing booth where they both exchanged a shilling for twelve pennies. Each selecting a one armed bandit, they simultaneously fed pennies into the coin slot and pulled down the machines handle. Several attempts later, the ching of copper hitting the metal payout cup brought a cheer from Alistair.

'Two cherries! That's eightpence!' he proclaimed excitedly.

'Ruddy hell, I thought you'd won the jackpot. Still, you go on boyo – It's better than a kick in the teeth. Ar've had nee luck yet,' sighed Billy as he fed another penny in the slot.

Lady luck hadn't completely deserted him though, because with his last coin, three lemons lined up, netting him one and sixpence.

'Yes me beauty! That's me in profit bonny lad,' he chortled, gleefully rubbing his hands together. 'Ar'll stick a shilling back in me sky rocket, an' then gamble me winnings. Ar canna lose.'

'Well done, Billy boy,' congratulated Alistair, putting his last penny into the machine. 'Hey up – a cherry! That's another fourpence. Let's see. . . ' he calculated. 'I should have broke even.' He counted his pennies. 'Yep, a shilling exactly. That's me finished. I'll watch you gamble yer winnings now Billy. Whatever 'appens, we've lost nowt.'

'That's the way to play these things, my little Yorkshire terrier. Some folks'll come on a day trip an' spend all their brass in an arcade. Best thing to dee is 'ave a little dabble. Then . . . win or lose, just walk away.'

'The sixpence Billy had won went back into the one armed bandit, but this time there was no return. 'Ah well, never mind, we've both lost nowt. Ha way, let's gan an' see if them two puffs 'ave finished preenin' themselves in the bog.'

'Come on Billy Fury, hurry up in that mirror,' demanded Roy. 'Ar want to look at my handsome mush.' Roy was drying his hands and face on some toilet paper, having had a wash, complaining all the while at the lack of hot water. Not that he was bothered anyway, the weather being so hot – The cold water had freshened him up nicely. He just liked to kick up a fuss.

'Get thee pipe man,' chided Stuart. 'Ar've got to look me best fer Laura. Some of us do pull the birds yer nar, an' don't just pretend to, an' then brag aboot it.'

'Get knotted lard heed. That Laura was eyeing me up first, but ar kept looking away, not giving her any encouragement like. Ar didn't want to disappoint Karen an' Sarah. Ar noticed 'em droolin' all ower me. Yer canna blame 'em like – they've certainly got good taste.'

'Oh aye! In yer dreams boy. If they fancy yer, how come yer've not copped off wi' one of 'em then?'

'Whey, that's simple milky . . . Ar divent fancy either of 'em. They're not good enough fer the likes o' me. As well you nar . . . my standards are very high.'

'Give ower. The only birds ye pull are scrubbers man.'

'Bollocks! Ar mean, these birds . . . They're too common man. How can yer gan out with a Yorkshire lass? Ee by gum, there's trouble at t' mill – an' all that lingo. Following a shite team like Leeds United – What's all that aboot? They've nee taste or class at all.'

'Shut up Roy! Just because they've given yer the elbow. Ar think they're good fun an' interesting, an' besides, most birds don't like football. They're probably keen on it because Katy plays,' he surmised. 'There's nowt wrong wi' lasses enjoying football, or playing it fer that matter. The more the merrier, as far as I'm concerned.'

'Ah . . . yer big ponce. Football's a man's game an' always will be. Netball's fer lasses . . . that an' rounders. Oh aye, an' not fergetting – mekking the beds an' hoovering the house.'

'They're not sports,' Stuart pointed out.

'Whey, yer nar what ar mean . . . girlie things.'

'Ar thought you liked netball an' rounders,' remarked Stuart.

'How d'yer mean?'

'Well, back at school, yer always round the girls netball court, watching 'em play. It wouldn't be the fact that they happen to be wearing short gym skirts would it?'

'Arraway an' shite man. Ar go round that part o' the school to meditate. Ar canna help it if there's lasses there at the same time. It's just coincidence man.'

'Anyway, ar divent nar how yer've got the cheek to slag off girls football after your performance today,' derided Stuart. 'That Katy showed yer how it's done. You're not fit to lace her boots man.'

Stuart certainly wasn't holding back today. He was even amazing himself by his outspokeness towards Roy. He felt like the Cock of the North.

'We are full of our sens today, aren't we lardy? You wanna watch yer sen boy,' Roy warned him, without much conviction.

'Yer heading fer a knuckle sandwich bonny lad. Ar mean, was it my fault ar got injured? No – an' just when ar was ganna score a stunner an' all. Yes . . . unfortunate for yers that. You all missed a lesson in the art of playing football. Alas, my skills were not to be shown. The loss is yours, I'm afraid . . . No lad, they divent call me the Stanhope Stanley Matthews fer nowt yer nar.'

'Bah . . . yer divent half come out with a right load o' shite.'

'Hey, watch it lad,' said Roy as he cuffed Stuart round the ear.

'Hooray . . . Here at last,' uttered the girls in dull monotones, accompanied with a sarcastic round of applause. They'd been standing waiting outside the toilets for quite some time.

'What the heck took you so long?' complained Karen.

'They'll 'ave been giving each other one,' muttered Billy to Alistair as they rejoined the group after their short spell in the arcade. 'The pair of woolly woofters,' he added causing Alistair to laugh.

'Alright, what's so funny like?' demanded Roy. 'If yer've owt to say, let's be 'aving it.'

'Keep yer 'air on – what yer've got,' chortled Billy. 'It's nowt, bonny lad, yer getting paranoid. Alistair was just saying like – That both of yers 'ave left yer flies undone.'

Roy and Stuart instinctively covered their crotch area with their hands as they looked down. Both were relieved to discover they'd zipped up correctly.

'Ha, ha! Had yer ganning there!' grinned Billy.

'Whey, aren't you just a barrel of laughs, Billy boy?' scoffed Roy. 'If yer must nar – Ar was waiting for Stuart to squeeze the pus out of his spots. If that wasn't bad enough, ar had to wash it off the mirror afore ar could use it to confirm my handsome face in my reflection.'

'Yuck! Shut up Roy, that's awful,' grimaced Sarah.

'What's awful, Stuart's zits? 'Cause yer canna mean my handsome looks are awful.'

'Both!' chorused the girls.

'Orh . . . Stuart doesn't 'ave spots, do yer love?' said Laura protectively stroking his cheek. 'His face is like a baby's bottom,' she added.

Stuart bristled, cockily sticking his chest out, chin held high, smirking at Roy. 'Well thank you Laura, but I feel I must take issue with you on one tiny significant point. Although of course my skin **is** flawless . . . I doubt that you did not fail to notice my manly stubble whilst caressing my face?'

'How could I have not been aware?' condescended Laura, playing along with Stuart's little charade. 'I had already noticed the look of envy on the face of your hedgehog headed friend, due to his lack of facial hair.'

'Arraway an' shite, yer sarcastic set of sods. Ar's off to be sick.' With that, Roy turned and went back into the toilets.

After much mirth and merriment from the others at Roy's expense, he rejoined them, chuntering away to himself as to why he allowed such infantile imbeciles the privilege of his company.

They strolled down the sea front, looking in shop windows, stopping at a rock and novelty shop.

'I'm treating me sen,' announced Katy, noticing some hats in the doorway. 'Anyone else coming in?' she asked as she entered the shop.

'I think I might buy one our lass,' said Laura, 'Wait for me.'

They all piled in the shop.

Cash register symbols lit up in the eyes of the proprietor, in anticipation of the potential trade about to take place.

'Have a good look round ladies and gentlemen,' he proffered, rubbing his hands together. 'I'm short of nothing. If you can't see what you require, just ask. I have a substantial store room, full of quality merchandise.'

'What a prat,' muttered Roy. 'It's a load of junk.'

'Do you ever stop complaining?' criticised Billy. 'Nowt's ever right where you're concerned.'

'Whey, ar's only telling the truth ginger heed.'

'Can we try them Kiss me Quick hats on please?' Katy asked the shopkeeper.

'You certainly can. And a good choice, if I may say so young lady. They're fine quality hats – the best in Whitley Bay. If you'll bear with me, I won't be a minute,' he said, disappearing under the counter.

'Is he for real?' whispered Stuart. 'What a creep.'

The shop keeper emerged with a small pair of steps which were neccessary to reach the display of hats above the shop doorway. The lads watched him in fascination, fussing about like a demented dwarf.

'If he's a full shilling, ar's a chinaman,' skitted Roy. 'An' ar divent think he is somehow. What a creepy slimeball. Are yer sure he's not related to you Alistair?'

'Ha ha, that is so funny . . . an' there I was thinking what a great partner he'd make for you,' retorted Alistair. 'Two peas in a pod, an' both round the bend.'

'Here you are ladies, try these fine hats on for size. There's a mirror for your convenience over in the corner,' the vendor informed them as he handed over an assortment of hats.

'Thank you,' giggled the girls, taking them from him.

'Now then gentlemen. Have you noticed anything that's caught your eye?'

'Not as yet,' Billy informed him.

'I have, muttered Roy, 'A load o' shite. There's more chance of me buying summat from a scrapyard than owt in this khazie.'

'Pardon me? I didn't quite catch what you said.'

'Whey, ar was just saying like – There's such an abundance of quality goods on view, I'm completely overwhelmed by it all,' said Roy in his usual facetious tone.

'Well, thank you for your complimentary remarks young man. It's always nice to see good manners in the youth of today.'

'Think nowt of it – my pleasure.'

'Well, by all means, continue to look for as long as you like. Just ask if you require my assistance. Now ladies, how are we doing with those hats?'

'He's definately not playing with a full deck,' commented Roy when the shopkeeper was safely out of earshot. 'He's a mentalist. Ar was tekking the piss, but he didn't cotton on. Daft bugger probably thinks he's running an offshoot of Harrods. Bloody coastal hillbilly.'

The other lads chuckled quietly. They did have some decorum, even if Roy didn't have.

'This rock's soft as shite! It must be ten years old at least man. Look at the lettering in it . . . HITLEY AY. Whey, it just gans to prove my point – he's selling seconds. Rock and novelty shop my arse. The old bugger'd be better off changing that sign to antique shop. His business'll boom then.'

'Stop complaining all the time,' admonished Alistair. 'The bloke's only doing his best to be helpful. You do what yer want, but I'm buying some rock fer me nana an' auntie Kitty. There's some good novelty rock over there,' he informed the rest of them. 'Look, there's dummies, an' plates of bacon an' eggs an' humbug rock . . . '

'Humbug,' sneered Roy. 'How appropriate – with a scrooge like that running the shop.'

'Listen to yer, you're too tight to buy owt fer anyone,' derided Alistair.

'Rubbish! It's common knowledge that ye Yorkshire folk are tight – along with the jocks. Yer wouldn't part with yer own shite if yer didn't 'ave to.'

Alistair selected three medium sized sticks of rock, thinking his grandad might appreciate one as well.

Stuart bought rock for his family and a sugar dummy for Laura.

Billy opted for a box of fudge to take home with him while Roy rummaged through a bargain bin, choosing three broken sticks of rock which had been taped together and reduced to half price.

'Whey, ar've seen it all now,' said Billy, shaking his head in disbelief. 'Ar thought you weren't ganna buy owt from this scrapyard? You're a two faced bugger. Yer've been getting on at Alistair aboot how tight Yorkshiremen are – then yer've the cheek to buy cheap, broken rock. It's ye that's the skinflint.'

'Get thee pipe, carrot top. Tell me what 'appens when yer get yer whole sticks o' rock home . . . '

'Just cut to the chase,' said Billy, 'ar haven't got the slightest idea what yer on aboot.'

'Whey, ar'll tell yer, if yer'll listen a minute. Once yer back in Stanhope, yer gan in the kitchen, get the rolling pin out o' the drawer, an' proceed to smash up yer rock into little pieces.

Whereas I buy mine already broken up for me. The fact that it's half price is irrelevant – ar's just being practical – unlike ye fools, paying full whack.'

'Arraway an' shite, hedgehog heed. Yer a miser – Just admit it man.'

'Nee chance, bonny lad. Prudent is the word yer looking for . . . prudent. You'll do well to remember it.'

Having paid for their purchases, they left the shop. The girls were already outside, giggling and swapping their newly bought hats.

'Right then girls, who's first?' grinned Roy.

'First for what?' asked Sarah, looking puzzled.

'Whey, it's obvious – a kiss, that's what. Yer nar . . . Kiss me quick hats?'

'In your dreams boy.'

'Yeah, dream on,' added Laura.

Karen and Katy ran off down the sea front after warning Roy to keep away.

'Come back girls! Yer nar yer want to, stop teasing . . . Come to uncle Roy. They divent call me the Stanhope kisser fer nowt yer nar!'

'I'd rather kiss a frog,' declared a horrified Sarah.

'Me an' all,' added Laura. 'Though if someone else were to ask me . . . '

Stuart tapped himself on the forehead, muttering to himslf, 'God I'm slow at times.' He made a beeline for Laura and without permission – gave her a big smacker on the lips.

'That was nice,' she said coyly. 'What's that aftershave you've got on? It smells lovely.'

'It's Old Spice,' he announced proudly.

'Old milk, more like,' murmured a disgruntled Roy.

'Do ar detect a touch of jealousy?' taunted Billy.

'Nee way ginger – Not my type man. Ar's after summat a little more sophisticated than these Yorky types.'

'Oh, it's nowt to do with 'em not 'aving owt to dee wi' you then?'

'Nar, nee way. Ar want summat wi' a bit o' class. Yer nar . . .

what talk proper like.'

'Whey yer'd better get a move on bristle heed. The day's nearly ower wi' already.'

'Divent worry, it's nee sweat bonny lad.'

Catching up with Karen and Katy down the sea front, they became aware of a low rumbling noise. The sound gradually built up to a roaring crescendo as it became obvious it was a convoy of rockers on their motor bikes. Some fifty or sixty machines, some with side cars, some carrying pillion pasengers. Honking their horns, waving and shouting at one another, hardly audible against the thunderous racket.

The girls waved at them, jumping up and down, shrieking excitedly. Laura dropped her arm suddenly, realising that she might be upsetting Stuart by making him jealous.

'You don't seem that enthusiastic our lass,' Katy mentioned. 'Anyone would think yer'd just got married to Stewpot.'

'He's a sensitive lad,' said Laura putting her arm round him. 'Aren't you love?'

'Whey aye, pet.'

'Ar divent nar what all ye girls are getting excited aboot,' sneered Roy. 'Those travelling grease balls weren't waving at you anyway, they were waving at Stuart. They probably thought he was one of their long lost tribe, out on the town.'

'Up yours,' retorted Stuart.

'Ar noticed when they were passing us, that you sneaked off into that shop doorway shitting yer sen.'

'Whey, you've more in common wi' bikers than me,' skitted Stuart. 'Them skid marks they've left behind'll match them in yer underpants.'

'Go on Stu!' cheered Laura. 'You tell 'im!'

'Cocky bugger today, aren't we milky?' derided Roy. 'Showing off just because yer've held a lasses hand – yer think yer it. Well, ar divent want to put a damper on yer day out. Far be it from me to be glib aboot your new found love . . . '

'Gan on,' Stuart interrupted. 'Ar's waiting fer the pun.'

'Ar see yer've read the script milky. Here gans . . . I am reliably informed here by young Ken – ar mean Katy – that Laura's short sighted. She's as blind as a bat an' canna see how ugly you really are. It's nothing personal mind, just an observation like.'

He'd rattled Laura's cage – she'd over heard him. 'Well, I can certainly manage to see how ugly **you** are, big mouth! There's nowt wrong wi' Stuart's looks, he's gorgeous. An' me eyes are not all that bad anyway – hedgehog head, so get knotted!'

Roy had done it again. Having stirred up yet another hornets nest, he was content. He stood there with a satisfied smirk across his silly face. 'The fish always tek the bait,' he thought smugly to himself.

'Divent tek nee notice of him Laura,' placated Stuart. 'He just lives to get folks backs up. Yer've got to feel sorry fer him really. With having nee personality himself like, he has to resort to slagging everyone off. It's sad really, when yer think aboot it.'

'How can yer stick up fer such a rude pillock as him? You are caring Stuart . . . '

'One must try to be benevolent to these lesser mortals, and dig deep inside for forgiveness,' he preached.

'Whey, yer as bad as each other ye two,' mocked Roy. 'But yer'll never surpass my brilliant speel . . . A good attempt mind.'

Chapter 10

They carried on their aimless stroll.

Laura jumped onto Stuart's back and wrapped her arms around his neck. 'Giddy up trigger!' she demanded, laughing and slapping him on the backside. To her surprise, he set off like a racehorse. Juddering about violently, she shrieked to be put down.

'Whey, yer big babby,' laughed Stuart as he did her bidding.

'I didn't know you were gonna race off with me like a lunatic!' she protested, slapping him across the back. 'Yer daft bugger. I only wanted a piggy back, not a ride on the Grand National!'

Another short walk brought them to a public garden with a grassed area where they sat down.

There was a kiosk in one corner, displaying a blackboard with an endless list of refreshments.

'Gan an' get us a bottle o' pop our kid,' ordered Roy, delving into his pocket.

'Oh, yeah . . . an' what did your last slave die of? Go an' get it yourself,' came Alistair's none too helpful reply.

'Arh . . . yer lazy git. After all the things ar dee fer you an' all.'

The girls lay and stretched themselves out on the grass, soaking up the sun.

'We'll 'ave a bottle of lemonade if you're going to the shop Alistair,' said Karen. 'Oh, an' four bags of crisps as well. Is that alright with you girls?'

They all agreed.

'Well, get your brass out then. We can't expect Alistair to pay fer it an' all.'

The lads decided on crisps and agreed to share a large bottle of pop. Stuart handed over his money and then lay down beside Laura. Billy and Roy coughed up their money.

'I'm gonna need a hand,' stated Alistair. 'Any volunteers? Come on lads – who's the strongest?'

Roy got to his feet, 'Whey, seeing as yer put it like that Yorky – ar's yer man.'

Stuart and Billy didn't contest the walking ego. They were quite happy to lay there in the warm sun and be waited on by the knob head Roy.

'Ha way Ali, let's gan an' get a drink. Ar's as dry as a dingo's donger. Ar wonder if they sell fags?' pondered Roy as they set off across the green.

Half a dozen people were in the queue ahead of them.

'Ar've spotted some cigarettes kidder,' said Roy standing on tiptoe, peering over the heads in front of him. 'That's me sorted bonny lad.'

Noticing the vacant look about him, Roy snapped his fingers in front of Alistair's face. 'Earth calling Yorkshire git, come in please . . . '

'What? . . . Oh, I was miles away. I was wondering what me grandad an' his mates'll be doing back at the club.'

'Whey, it wouldn't tek a brain surgeon to work that one out, daft lad. They'll be knocking back the beer like there's nee tomorrow. No nagging wives giving 'em an ear bashing . . . While the cat's away . . . Aye, they'll be **lapping** it up. They 'ave to mek the most of it 'cause the ball an' chain'll be back on in the morning. Ar can just see 'em . . . coming round from a drunken stupor, dreaming they're momentarily free . . . Only to be brought back down to earth with a bang when the old battle-axe barges into the bedroom, her mouth ganning ten to the dozen. 'Are yer ganna stay in that pit all day? Come on, it's seven o'clock!' She'll then whip open the curtains so as the sun's shining on his pickled cranium. 'It smells like a bleeding midden in 'ere. Ar divent nar what they put in that beer down the club!' 'I do . . . watter,' he'll mumble into his pillow. 'What was that? Speak up man!' she'll demand. 'Ar said, ar's just coming pet.' 'Whey, mek sure yer are –

there's jobs to dee. Ar need some tatties digging up an' that lawn needs mowing. Come on, move yer sen!'

Alistair chuckled at Roy's mimicry.

'Ar tell yer what Ali, there's nee chance o' me getting married. If ar change me mind in the future, yer've got my permission to shoot me.'

'Is that a promise? Can I have it in writing?'

'Sure yer can, but yer'll never need it. Ar'll tell yer what though, my little Yorkshire pudding – If dildoes could mow lawns, it'd mek men redundant. There's nee doubt aboot that.'

Alistair was doubled in two laughing. On this occasion, he'd actually found Roy funny.

'What time is it now?' murmured Roy, looking at his watch. 'Half past four . . . They'll 'ave sank a gallon of ale by this time. More, some of 'em. The arguments'll be brekking out now wi' the beer talking. They'll each be accusing the other o' cheating at darts an' doms. Another five pints an' it'll be like the Battle o' Little Big Horn. The domino table'll be flying through the air . . . dominos scattered all ower. People walking aboot wi' darts sticking out o' the back o' their heeds. The glass collecter'll be wearing his crash helmet . . . Ar tell yer – it's serious man.'

'Come off it . . . You do exaggerate a bit.'

'It's all true bonny lad, ar swear it,' insisted Roy, his fingers crossed behind his back.

'I never knew people could sup that much beer in one go,' remarked Alistair shaking his head in disbelief. 'You'd think the club would run out of ale.'

'Whey, there's nee chance of that man. When they gan fer a slash, it's not wasted yer nar. It gets piped down to the cellar an' back into the barrels. Then it's pumped back up to the bar fer re-selling. Nee body cottons on, they're that drunk. Anyway, according to the regulars – the beer's like piss all o' the time, so they divent notice any difference. Ar tell yer what kidder . . . Ar'd love to be a fly on the wall in that 'men only' bar. There'll be plenty o' bullshite to listen in on, you can be certain o' that.'

'Men only . . . ' pondered Alistair. 'Does that mean there's no women allowed in that room?'

'By, there's nowt gets past you Sherlock. Course they're not allowed in, hence the name. Mind . . . No, ar tell a lie – They do stretch the rules a teeny bit an' allow one bird in. She works behind the bar, washing glasses an' mopping the floor – What women were put on this earth for. She canna talk to the customers though . . . Whey, yer divent want 'em to get above their station like. Keep 'em deeing the menial work, skivvying an' the like – that's all they're fit for . . . Whey, that an' a good seeing to now an' again. What else do they want? They divent nar they're born man . . . '

'You're unbelievable Roy!' gasped Alistair. 'They've abolished slavery yer know.'

'Aye, more's the pity,' Roy uttered.

'When is it the men have their club outing?' asked Alistair. 'I know it's not long after our trip.'

'Whey, it's aboot a fortnight after Stanhope show – The last week in September, bonny lad. Ar canna wait until ar's eighteen an' able to go with 'em. Now that'll be a right eye opener . . . An experience not to be missed . . . aboard the nutters express. Wrong choice of word there – express. Me grandfavver always says that wherever they gan, it teks five or six hours to get there. Apparently, 'cause they sup that much ale, the coach 'as to keep stopping every few miles to let 'em off fer a piss. Crates o' beer are nee good to them, the amount they knock back . . . The coach wouln't tek the weight, it'd knacker t' suspension up man.'

'Well, what do they do fer booze then?'

'Whey, a brewery wagon follows behind the coach. It tops 'em up throughout the journey. Do yer nar? Twenty percent of Newcastle an' Scottish Breweries stock gans to Stanhope Working Mens Club alone? They give everyone a free barrel o' beer at Christmas. Not only that . . . Every year the brewery lays on a free day trip fer 'em. They're spoilt rotten man.'

'Where do they go for the trip? Blackpool, Morecambe, Whitley Bay?' asked Alistair going along with Roy's banter, not knowing which was truth or fiction.

'The seaside? Them? Nee bonny lad. John Smiths Brewery in Tadcaster. Talk aboot tekking coals to Newcastle . . . They 'ave a quick tour round with a guide showing 'em how ale's brewed. One or two'll pretend to show a little interest, just to be diplomatic like . . . But they're only there fer the beer – it's free after the tour. Sandwiches are laid on as well. All courtesy of Scottish and Newcastle Brewery. It seems daft tekking 'em to another brewery, but Newcastle an' Scottish reckon it's to let 'em taste inferior beer to theirs.'

'And is it inferior?'

'Nar, they love it, but they dinna tell them that do they? They tell' em they think it's shite. They're not ganna spoil a good thing are they? They may be stupid, but not totally. A drivers mate gans along with 'em an' all yer nar.'

'What, just to go to Tadcaster?' exclaimed Alistair, trying to make his interest in Roy's banter sound plausible.

'Whey, it's not because they need two drivers . . . It's because it teks two of 'em to stretcher the piss heads back onto the coach.'

Roy was now becoming impatient in the queue. 'Bah, they're slow serving here. We've been here that long, we should've brought sleeping bags.'

'There's only two in front of us now, get thee pipe Geordie.'

'Ar've telt yer afore Yorky, we're Weardalers an' not Geordies – but yer nar that divent yer, clever dick? You're . . . '

Roy's forthcoming lecture was interrupted by the loudly ringing bell of a fire engine that was going at some speed down the promenade.

''Ave yer seen that kidder? It's ganning like the clappers. They love all that he-man shite them firemen. They're probably just ganning to rescue a cat stuck up a tree, the set o' puffs. Ar mean, what's all that aboot back at the station? They sit there, dossing aboot all day, playing cards, scoffing their faces . . . Then, when the alarm gans off, it's a race to the pole. They slide down it, like shit off a shovel – sandwiches still stuck in their gobs. What a carry on . . . Ar divent nar why they divent just buy a bungalow an' 'ave done with it. There'd be no need fer all that pole shite then.'

'It'd be a different tale if you ever had to be rescued by one of them,' reproached Alistair. 'Yer'd sing a different tune then.'

'Whey, ar wouldn't rely on Stanhope fire brigade, that's fer sure. They're all geriatrics man. It teks 'em half an hour to get assembled. By the time that they reached yer – yer'd 'ave either put the fire out yerself, or been burnt to a cinder. An' that fire engine's that old, it's still run on steam man.'

'Yes, young men, what can I get you?' smiled the pleasant female assistant at the counter.

'Nar then, what was it we wanted Yorky?' said Roy looking puzzled and scratching his head. 'We've been that long in this queue, ar can't remember. Two bottles of lemonade . . . an' how many bags o' crisps do we want?'

'Eight,' stated Alistair.

'Two bottles of lemonade, eight bags o' crisps an' ten Cadets tipped please.'

'How old are you?' asked the assistant.

'Ar's sixteen!' declared Roy indignantly.

'What's your date of birth then?'

'Fifth of June 1947,' he announced confidently, thinking smugly to himself that you'd have to be up early to catch him.

'Go on then, I'll believe you,' she said taking a packet of cigarettes from the shelf.

'Ar should hope you do believe me. They divent call me honest Roy fer nowt yer nar.'

'Yes yes, whatever . . . '

Alistair mouthed to the assistant from behind his hand, 'He's round the bend.'

She smiled at him and handed Roy his change.

'Here yer are Ali, cop fer these crisps. Ar'll tek the pop – ar divent want yer to strain that little pecker o' yours – giving yer self a hernia.'

'Get knotted!'

They set off back to the others, Alistair precariously carrying the crisps so as not to crush them.

'Divent drop any kidder,' advised Roy, 'Or yer winna get yer Crackerjack pencil,' he chuckled.

The others were laid out sunbathing with their eyes closed, Billy using the football as a pillow. Their peace was to be short lived.

'Wakey, wakey girls and boys! It's pop an' crisp time – you lucky people! There's a five shilling service charge mind,' added Roy.

'Aboot time an' all. Where've yer been for 'em,' complained Billy, 'Seaton Carew?'

'Whey, that's gratitude for yer. Stop yer moaning,' said Roy, throwing a packet of crisps at him.

The girls took one of the bottles of lemonade and each enjoyed a long welcome drink before passing it on to the next girl.

Roy gulped down a large swig of his bottle, and then passed it on before tucking into his bag of crisps. 'Bah, these crisps are soggy,' he grumbled. 'They're soft as shite man – probably got 'em from Stanhope Club.'

'Don't you ever stop complaining about everything?' rebuked Karen.

'Course ar dee bonny lass. When ar's asleep.'

'I'd like to put 'im to sleep ... permanently,' murmured Sarah.

'I think we all would,' added Laura.

'Do you want **another** one of my cigs Billy?' offered Roy. 'Ar nar yer divent like buying any like.'

'Gan on then, yer've twisted me arm. Cheers Roy ... owt fer nowt.'

Roy and Alistair sat themselves down with the rest of them. Roy put on his sunglasses before stretching himself prostrate on the grass.

'Ar divent nar aboot wearing sunglasses hedgehog head,' skitted Billy, 'But yer wanna get that bald heed of yours covered up. It's ganning as red as a baboons arse.'

'Huh! Ye've no room to talk, ginger nut. At least ar's not covered in freckles. Yer could do with a carrier bag on your heed. It's well known that ye freaks o' nature aren't suited to the sun. Enjoy that cig an' all – It's the last one you'll be geting from me.'

Billy gave Roy the V sign.

'You an' all,' returned Roy, using the same gesture.

A short period of peace and quiet descended on the group as they lay in the sun, some of them even drifting off into a light slumber, which was soon broken by a restless Roy's big mouth.

'Ha way! Wakey wakey! Time's knocking on boys and girls. Yer'd better start getting yer sens ready fer the off. Ar winna be long – ar's just nipping off fer a jimmy riddle.'

'Yer don't 'ave to go into detail,' objected Sarah sitting up and tidying her hair. 'We get the message thank you.'

'Quick,' said Katy grinning, 'Let's get going while knob head's at the toilet.'

'Tempting as that is,' agreed Alistair, 'But we'd better wait for him. I'd never hear the last of it. He'd be moaning in me lug hole all the way home on the bus.'

Katy shook Laura, 'Laura, wake up! Come on our lass, we're off to the toilet.'

Laura opened her eyes, momentarily getting her bearings. You could've gone without me, I was enjoying that kip. I wouldn't 'ave run off an' left you little sister.'

Stuart woke from his nap. He yawned and looked at his watch. 'Nearly five o'clock,' he stated. 'Where's the day gone? It's always the same when yer enjoying yerself – time just flies by. 'Ave yer ever noticed that? If yer bored or miserable, it drags by. Funny that . . . '

The girls went to the ladies to freshen up, passing Roy as he came out of the gents.

'Hey up girls! Mek sure yer divent splash yer shoes in that bog.'

The girls preferred to ignore his comment, and went straight into the ladies.

'What a tosser he is,' derided Sarah. 'I'll miss him like a boil on the bum.'

'I'll second that,' agreed Karen. 'Talk about being overbearing, he certainly takes the biscuit. Still, never mind . . . Laura's found her true love in Stuart. Will you be coming home with us Laura or are yer gonna elope with Stewpot to Gretna green?'

Laura pretended to act dreamily, 'Do you know . . . ? I might just do that . . . On second thoughts though,' she grinned, 'I can't leave our Katy on her own – she wouldn't survive two minutes without me.'

'Course I would,' objected Katy. 'I think you'll find it's the other way round, an' you'll be lost without me more like,' she insisted.

'I don't think so little sister. For starters, you'd hardly have any clothes to wear. Come on, be honest – you borrow mine all the time – don't deny it.'

'Maybe I do,' admitted Katy. 'But you've got that many clothes, it's a shame not to mek use of 'em. An' as for shoes . . . Do you know? She's got that many pairs of shoes in her bedroom, it's like Stead an' Simpson's in there . . . I'm not joking.'

'Well, so what?' maintained Laura. 'You're addicted to fruit machines – I'm addicted to shoes. Nowt wrong in that.'

'Correction, I **used** to be addicted to fruit machines – There's the difference.'

Having finished their ablutions, the girls left the ladies feeling somewhat fresher.

'Bloody hell!' exclaimed Roy. 'We thought you'd got lost. Stuart was ganna send out a search party to look for yers. He only stopped crying when he saw yer coming ower the green.'

'Give it a rest motor mouth!' retorted Stuart.

Roy smirked contentedly, his statement having had the desired effect.

'Is that a chewing gum machine outside that shop over there Alistair?' asked Katy.

'Yeah, it's a Beechnut one. There's an Arrowmint one round the other side, an' a gobstopper machine as well. Get one o' them fer our Roy while yer there will yer?'

'Don't yer think two'll be better?' she skitted.

'Aye, yer probably right there,' chuckled Alistair.

'My ears are burning,' said Roy, suddenly aware of the surreptitious looks he was receiving.

'Well get some hair grown over 'em then,' stated Alistair grinning. 'It'll protect 'em from the sun,' he sniggered.

'Yer nar what ar mean Yorky, there's nee need to be clever. You're getting above yer station boyo.'

'That's rich, coming from you.'

After asking if anyone else wanted anything from the shop, Katy ran off across the grass. She examined each chewing gum machine in turn, and smiling to herself, selected the Beechnut one. Placing a penny in the slot, she turned the knob on the side of the machine and two packets of chewing gum were deposited. Luck was with her again . . . The etched arrow on the knob had been pointing forward – hence the extra packet. She wasn't nick named King Midas at school for nothing.

'I bet anyone ten bob,' surmised Laura, 'Our Ken comes back with a free packet. I've never known anyone as lucky as her. If she fell in a barrel of shit, she'd come out smelling of roses. I'll tell yer summat – When we're old enough to do the pools, I'm definately sharing with her.'

Katy rejoined the group, a wide grin on her face.

'I knew it!' exclaimed Laura. 'Go on, tell us what yer've wangled fer nowt this time.'

'Just a packet of Beechnut, nowt to write home about sis,' she shrugged, casually. 'I was going to get a gobstopper fer Roy, but there wasn't one big enough so I didn't bother.'

They all chuckled, suffice to say except for Roy, who was not amused at all, and snapped at Katy, 'Divent ye start, tomboy. Ar tell the funnies round here, young 'en,' he snarled.

'You could've fooled us,' derided Karen.

Roy carried on his onslaught at Katy, 'Just because yer can dribble a football a bit – divent let it gan to yer heed. Ar mean, what future's in that fer a girl? It's not as if yer can dee an apprenticeship in football an' gan on and play fer England. Granted . . . yer'll be able to turn out fer Leeds United 'cause they're a load o' women anyway. They certainly play like big girls.'

'They're better than that Sunderland rubbish anyday,' stated an indignant Katy, trying to appear calm, thus not giving Roy any smug satisfaction.

'Whey, even the Derby an' Joan club's better than Sunderland,' interrupted Billy. 'So ar'd keep quiet it ar was ye Roy – especially after your performance with the football on the beach bonny lad.'

Roy protested unconvincingly, 'Ar've telt yer afore . . . ar couldn't perform my magic football skills because of my injury.'

'Aye, an' pigs might fly.'

Karen looked at her watch, 'Well girls, it's nearly time we were off,' she announced. 'We don't want to miss the coach, do we?'

'You speak for yourself,' said Laura glumly.

'Well, we all know that you don't want to go home, but yer've no choice I'm afraid,' she stated, a little sympathetically.

'Where's yer coach parked?' asked Stuart. 'Is it far?'

'No, it's not far from here,' replied Laura. 'It's about forty yards down the prom an' up a side street. Where's yours?'

'Just a bit further on. It canna be more than a quarter of a mile,' he added, trying to sound chirpy while deep down he was really feeling dreadful at the thought of his separation with Laura. He took hold of her hand and led her away from the rest of the group to a stone wall where they sat down.

Karen shouted after them, 'Don't be long, or we'll miss the coach!'

'Good,' muttered Laura, before shouting back, 'Okay, I won't be long!'

Laura and Stuart had a quiet chat, exchanged addresses and then returned to the group.

'Right then! All present and correct ladies and gentlemen? Let's get ganning then,' heralded Roy, taking charge – or so he thought, but no one was taking a blind bit of notice of him. 'Mek sure yer've left nowt behind. Ye can carry the football Yorky, seeing as yer the youngest. Ar'll carry the rock.'

'Don't you strain yerself will yer?' skitted Alistair.

They left the green, Stuart and Laura feeling sorry for themselves, slowly walking hand in hand behind the rest of them, knowing that in a few minutes they would be going their own separate ways.

Stuart said with a lump in his throat, 'Whey, ar've had a great day, but all good things must come to an end.'

'They reckon this weather's gonna last for quite a while yet,' commented Laura. 'I wish we could stay for the week.'

'Aye, me too . . . Mebbe if we keep in touch, we could organise a week together next year,' said Stuart enthusiastically, knowing full well that in a few weeks time, or even a few days, their day trip romance would soon become a memory. 'Still . . . you never know . . . ' he thought to himself.

Back on the sea front, a welcome breeze now greeted them.

'By, that's a grand wind,' said Roy. 'Hey, up Alistair, yer'd better hold on to yer syrup o' fig – Yer divent want it blowing away.'

'You're only jealous because I've got plenty of hair,' retorted Alistair, turning his back against the increasing wind.

'It might be a nice cool breeze, but I'm getting sand in me face,' said Sarah, spitting some out of her mouth.

'An' I've got it in me eyes,' added an irritated Katy.

'Serves yer right Yorkies,' boasted an arrogant Roy, adjusting his sunglasses. 'Yer should've come prepared like me, an brought some sunglasses.' He turned his attentions to a blackboard outside a fish and chip shop. 'Ar divent nar where they get these prices from,' he observed as he scrutinised the price list. Have yer ever wondered why fish an' chips always cost a fortune at the seaside? Ar mean – the fish are only fifty yards away. Any nearer an' they'd probably jump out of the sea themselves, straight into the frying pan. It's just a bloody rip off. They're that much cheaper to buy inland – even though there's the cost of refridgeration an' transport . . . It's weird that, divent yer think?' Roy looked round, waiting for some reaction to uphold his words of wisdom, but none was forthcoming. Unperturbed, he carried on, 'Even Harold's chippy, back in Stanhope is cheaper than at the coast, an' that bugger's fish an' chips are the dearest in Durham.'

'What a boring prat he is,' muttered Katy to Sarah. 'Going on about the price of fish an' chips. He's like an old washer woman. Thank God we'll be seeing the back of him soon.'

'Aye, he's been the only thing that's spoilt the day,' commented Sarah. 'We've had a brilliant day though, 'aven't we Ken? Apart from knob head.'

'Aye, ar've right enjoyed me sen yer nar, bonny lass,' mimicked Katy. 'There's nee doubt aboot it hinny . . . An' stop calling me Ken.'

The sea front was quiet now. Most daytrippers were back at their coaches, ready for the journey home. Folks that were staying for the next week or two, would now be tucking into their evening meal back at their 'digs.'

Having arrived at the side street where the girls coach was parked, they said their farewells.

'Well, ar would just like to say what a great pleasure it's been for you girls to have had the privilege of my company for the day. A great honour in itself,' proclaimed Roy.

'What is he on?' ridiculed Sarah.

'Positivity my dear . . . Positivity . . . ' declared Roy, adopting a W C Fields stance and adding, 'My little chick-a-dee . . . '

'Well, I'm certainly positive,' assured Sarah. 'Positive I won't be seeing you again.'

Roy shrugged his shoulders, 'Whey, it's your loss, my little Yorkshire terrier. Your lives will be all the duller now after a day spent in the presence of my good self. Any future outings you participate in will pale into insignificance after the day you chose to spend in my acquaintance. Divent be thanking me though, there's no need. My reward in bringing untold joy into the world, is ample enough.'

'That's it – he's gone completely doolally,' stated Karen. 'Come on girls, time to go. Cheerio lads.'

'See yer girls,' echoed the lads as they turned to leave.

'Same time, same place next year!' called Roy.

'Over my dead body,' scorned Sarah.

Stuart and Laura lingered behind, stealing a last kiss and cuddle.

'Come on our lass!' bellowed Katy. 'You'll miss the bus!'

Laura gave Stuart one last kiss and left him unwillingly, running off to catch up with the others, fighting back the tears – a feeling of utter desolation inside her.

Stuart too, felt empty inside, but he couldn't let his feelings be known to the others. Taking a deep breath, he set off in pursuit of catching them up. 'Phew, women! Yer canna get away from 'em. Well, at least I can't,' he boasted, decreeing that boasting was his best form of defence in the event of an attack from Roy.

Roy took the bait. 'Huh! Have yer heard lover boy? He cops off with a Yorkshire 'eeh by gum' bird an' thinks he's Gods gift to women. He'll be walking aboot Stanhope next fer months on end, in a flat cap wi' a whippet on a piece o' string.' Roy glanced towards Stuart expecting some response, but he was disappointed.

Roy's sarcasm wasn't even registering with him. His thoughts were with Laura and their blissful time spent together. His heart was pining more than he ever thought possible.

'Hey! Billy Fury, wake up!' bawled Roy, snapping his fingers in front of Stuart's face. 'Divent be ganning all soppy on us ower a bird – especially a Yorkshire one. They're all as rough as a bears arse man. That's why ar declined their advances, even though they were extremely persistent. Yer probably noticed how ar'd 'ave nowt to dee with 'em. Definately not classy enough fer my high standards.'

Stuart wasn't taking a blind bit of notice of Roy's bullshit, preferring instead to remain in his dreamworld . . .

Billy had not failed to notice however. 'By, what a load o' drivel ye come out with!' he exclaimed. 'You didn't get a look in man. Them lasses soon had you weighed up, an' then kept well away from yer, as well you know it! They divent call yer the Stanhope reject fer nowt yer nar.'

'Arraway an' shite carrot heed,' argued Roy. 'Both Karen **and** Sarah desired my company fer the day, saying ar was the best looking lad in Whitley Bay. Ar had to let 'em down gently like. Ar declined quietly, without any fuss ar might add. Yer see, ar didn't want to embarrass the girls in front of all an' sundry. Besides . . . ' he added, 'They were ugly.'

'Yer lying bugger! They were all good lookers! That's why yer never got near 'em,' derided Billy. 'You stick to yer usual scrubbers. Them Yorkshire lasses were out o' your league man. That reminds me . . . You've not pulled a bird today . . . You've got to show yer arse in Burton's window, remember?'

'Divent be silly, Billy. Ar was only joking man. Yer dinna think ar'd be that childish do yer? Grow up ginger, yer worse than a two year old.' Roy was inwardly squirming, his fingers crossed behind his back, hoping and praying he'd wriggle out of his predicament.

'It's not your lucky day is it Roy?' sniggered Billy, an evil mischievous grin on his face. 'Ha way lads – Let's de-bag the git.'

De-bagging meant pulling his trousers down below his knees.

Alistair and Stuart stepped forward to join in the jovial jape.

'No, give ower, yer set o' pillocks,' protested Roy. 'Ar've got skid marks on me underpants. Yer'll show me up man!' he pleaded.

They managed to pin him to the ground after a short struggle.

'Hold him still if yer can lads,' said Billy. 'Ar'll get his kecks off.'

'Behave yer sen man – yer'll dee me an injury!' wailed Roy.

Billy took no notice and proceeded with the de-bagging. He sat on Roy's shins and undid his trouser buttons before pulling them down to his knees. 'Urgh, look! exclaimed Billy. 'His undies are all yellow with piss!' he lied, and then ran off down the sea front with Alistair and Stuart, laughing their socks off.

'You set of bas . . . . . ' Roy checked himself, 'baskets!' he shouted. 'Ar'll get yer back fer this, divent ye worry!' he threatened, pulling his pants up.

'No, we won't worry!' Billy shouted back.

They crossed the main road onto the promenade. With all the tom foolery going on, Stuart's sadness had waned temporarily. A sombre mood descended on him once again.

Chapter 11

Their coach came into view. As they approached it, they could see their fellow passengers sitting around on benches. Some were leaning against the promenade railings, enjoying their last chance of the sun. Some kids were swinging on the railings, while others were running amock around the two stationary coaches, resulting in a severe telling off from Alf.

'Hey up lads, wait for me!'

They turned to see Roy crossing the road, heading towards them. 'Yer set o' rotten sods,' he grumbled as he caught them up. 'Yer put me in a right predicament. When ar stood up to pull me kecks back up, I got accosted. A gang o' lasses were passing by an' they must 'ave seen the large bulge in me underpants because they mobbed me. They were like a pack o' wild animals man. Ar heard one of 'em shout, 'It's Errol Flynn!' Another shouted, 'Look at the size of him!' Ar must admit mind – it was a bit scary. If it hadn't been fer a shop keeper coming to me rescue, they'd 'ave got at me John Thomas. It was a narrow escape. Me underpants are in shreds.'

'Yes Roy,' tutted Billy. 'We believe you.'

The lads were thinking how well Roy had responded to the de-bagging, and therefore smelt a rat. Roy was a cunning bugger. They'd best be alert for the journey home – There was no telling what he had up his sleeve.

'Ar's not looking forward to the journey home,' announced Roy. 'That antique coach of ours'll be like a giant furnace. An' as fer all them smelly little kids chelping on aboot what they did an' didn't do today – it doesn't bear thinking aboot.'

'It won't be that bad,' assured Billy. 'They'll start off – their gobs ganning ten to the dozen, but it doesn't last long. The sea air . . . the energetic day, plus the rocking of the coach . . . It'll soon put 'em to sleep.'

'Rocking of the coach?' exclaimed Roy. 'Bloody hell, if that old banger gans ower a match stick, yer heed hits the roof.'

'Stop exaggerating Roy,' rebuked Alistair. 'It's not such a bad ride. Rocks me to sleep anyway. Gives me a break from listening to you complaining all the time.'

'Rocks me to sleep . . . ' derided Roy in a childish voice. 'Whey, it would dee, yer great Yorkshire puff.'

'Alright Geordie, there's no need fer insults. Just because yer got de-bagged . . . ' sniggered Alistair.

'Aye, yer set of twats. Divent think ar'll ferget that in a hurry an' all. My turn will come . . . that's fer sure.'

'Yes Roy,' sighed Billy. 'We're shaking in ower boots. Me underpants have got skid marks – just like yours.'

'Get stuffed.'

As they approached the two coaches, Alistair, a short step ahead of the rest, stopped in his tracks. 'Blooming heck!' he exclaimed. 'Have yer seen me nana an' auntie Kitty? Look! On that bench over there,' he indicated.

'Bloody hell! There's four of 'em. They look like boiled lobsters!' laughed Roy. 'Looks like this journey home could be fun after all.'

Trying their best to keep straight faces, the boys walked up to nana, Kitty, Mabel and Betty.

'Yer've gone a bit ower board with the rouge, 'aven't yer ladies?' smirked Roy.

'Bugger off!' retorted nana.

It was no good, the lads couldn't contain themselves any longer. They burst out laughing at the comical sight. Even Stuart joined in – miserable as he was.

'Robins are early this year,' chortled Billy.

'Divent ye start an' all, yer cheeky monkey!' chastised Kitty.

Roy, couldn't resist another snipe at the four sunburnt women.

'Yer nar, if you all stood together, yer'd look like four matches – fat ones like, ar'll grant yer.'

'Watch it, bugger lugs,' warned Betty. 'You're not too old fer a clip round the lug 'ole.'

'Whey, what 'appened fer yer to look like four blood oranges?' asked Roy.

'We fell asleep in our deck chairs if yer must nar,' nana informed him. 'Happy now?'

'Alright nana, divent get all **hot headed.**' Roy just couldn't help himself.

'Divent push yer luck.'

'Whey, ar mean – Tell us why yer went to sleep in the sun. Yer always lecturing me an' our Alistair aboot the dangers of the sun.'

'Aye that's true lad, but when we sat down fer our afternoon siesta, we were in the shade. We woke up in the sun.'

'Bah, my head's fair thumping,' groaned Betty, putting her hand to her forehead. 'Ar's not used to boozing like that.'

'Ah . . . so yer were all drunk,' said Roy grinning. 'That's why yer slept through the sun burning yer. Ar've nee sympathy for yer.'

'We were tiddly, not drunk son,' reproached his mother.

'Pull the other leg it's got bells on.'

Mabel removed her hat and wiped her brow with a handkerchief. She looked up with bemusement as every one burst out laughing.

'What's so funny?' she questioned indignantly.

'Eeh, lass . . . Yer look a sight,' laughed Mabel, wiping the tears from her eyes. 'Yer've got a white ring on yer forehead where yer hat's been.'

'Oh, is that all. Ar thought ar'd grown another heed or summat, the way yer carrying on.' Mabel then started chuckling when she realised how she must look.

'All aboard the Stanhope Express!' bellowed Alf.

'Aye, let's be 'aving yer!' added Bert. 'Five minutes an' we want to be off.'

'Express!' exclaimed Roy. 'Who do they think they're kidding? Ar've seen faster milk floats . . . perhaps with the exception of

Billy Fury's there,' he said, nodding in the direction of Stuart.

There was no reaction from Stuart, who just couldn't be bothered with Roy's glibness at this moment in time.

Kids clamoured to the coaches, all fighting to get on board, only to be stopped in their tracks by Alf and Bert who then let them on in an orderly fashion, one at a time.

Some women and children were only just making their way from the beach, having heard Alf and Bert's call.

'Ye lads get on the coach an' secure our seats,' instructed Kitty. 'We'll follow yer.'

Roy was first on the coach, naturally.

'Hey up lads. 'Ave yer had a good day?' inquired Alf.

'Aye, it's been canny like,' replied Billy cordially. 'We could nee ask fer better weather like.'

'It wasn't bad ar suppose,' sighed Roy, nonchalantly as he hauled himself onboard. 'Only trouble was, the lack of classy chicks, they weren't up to my high standards. Ar'll tell yer what Alf,' said Roy changing the subject, 'The pollace'll 'ave yer one o' these days fer that yer nar.'

'Ar divent have the slightest clue what yer on aboot bonny lad,' said a puzzled Alf.

'Whey, ar's referring to that Guiness label yer've got stuck on the windscreen where yer tax disc should be. It's been there three years to my knowledge.'

'Arraway with yer,' chuckled Alf, cuffing Roy round the ear. 'It's up to date as well you know.'

Roy ran down the bus like a two year old, making sure he got his window seat. He sat down smugly, well satisfied. Alistair sat directly in front of Roy, while Billy and Stuart sat adjacent to Alistair.

'Be like that Yorky! It doesn't bother me, yer sitting on yer own, but me nana an' me mother'll soon shift yer out o' their seat.' Roy noticed an apple core stuffed in the ash tray in front of him. The penny dropped . . . He'd only gone and sat in the wrong seat. He looked up to see a youngster standing in the aisle.

'Mummy, mummy, that nasty boy's in my seat.'

Roy stood up. 'Watch yer mouth, yer little prat,' he muttered as he sidled past him, 'Or ar'll give yer a kick up the backside.'

The other lads laughed as Roy sat down next to Alistair.

'Alright alright, settle down girls. Anyone can make a mistake. Stop acting like a set o' bairns.'

Molly and Kitty climbed aboard as Mabel and Betty went to get on Bert's coach in front.

'Come on ladies. Last as usual,' teased Alf. 'What yer been up to? Yer like a couple of betroots.'

'Oh, divent ask man,' said an irritated Molly, 'Suffice to say that we went to sleep in the shade . . . and woke up in the sun.'

'Was that before or after yer'd been to the boozer?' questioned Alf.

'After,' admitted Kitty. 'We only had a couple o' shandies mind.'

'Arraway with yer. Yer nowt but a couple o' drunks. Ar hope yer not ganna misbehave on my bus.'

'Never mind us bugger lugs, we're not the ones driving. Come ower 'ere an' let me smell yer breath,' ordered nana.

Alf breathed out, humouring Molly. 'Satisfied now are we?'

'Whey, all ar could smell was peppermints. Ar hope yer not sucking 'em to hide the smell of beer.'

'Eeh . . . Molly lass, yer've hurt my feelings. Casting aspersions like that on my flawless character. Shame on you. How could you doubt my word?'

'Ar'll give yer the benefit of the doubt – just this once mind,' emphasised Molly. 'An' think on – drive carefully,' she added.

'Yes madam, your wish is my command,' he said, bowing.

The lads tried to suppress their laughter once again as they saw nana and Kitty making their way down the bus.

'Gan on, get it out of yer systems!,' barked Kitty. 'We can all get some peace then, with a bit o' luck.'

Neither nana or Roy's mother were in the best of moods. The sun had definately got to them. All they wished for now was a nice sleep on the journey home.

'All present and correct!' declared Alf after walking down the coach doing a head count. 'Only ten minutes late an' all – must be a record. We'll just get cranked up an' then we'll be on our way.'

A few muffled cheers went up from the tired kids.

'If anybody sees a moth flying aboot, divent kill it!' announced Roy. 'That's the air conditioning!'

It brought a laugh from the women but obviously went straight over the kids heads.

'It's ower hot in here Alf man.'

'Divent sweat Roy lad. Once we get ganning there'll be a right breeze blowing through them windows.'

'Not at the speed ye gan at,' murmured Roy.

At a quarter past six, the two coaches pulled out and headed for home.

Contrary to Roy's fears of a noisy journey, it was relatively quiet. The hot sunny day had taken it's toll, leaving the atmosphere in the coach unusually subdued. Only a matter of minutes into their journey, there was total quiet.

'Alistair . . . ' whispered Roy.

'What!' snapped Alistair, unhappy at being disturbed just as he was drifting off into the land of nod.

'Do yer nar? There's twice as many eyebrows in the world than there is people.'

'Very interesting Roy. Now give yer mouth a rest an' let me go to sleep.'

'Alright Yorky, keep yer 'air on.'

Alistair closed his eyes once more and reflected back on the days events. It hadn't been Roy's day had it? In fact, he'd been the butt of all the jokes. Getting a taste of his own medicine for a change . . . Yes – there'd been lots of laughs. A good day all round . . . and with Stanhope Show only weeks away, he had that to look forward to. He felt very contented as he drifted off to sleep. 'Aye, this'll dee me . . . '